Maiden of Orleans

Best Wishes!
Joe Rogers

MAIDEN OF ORLEANS

A Bayou Thriller

Joseph Patrick Rogers

iUniverse, Inc.
New York Lincoln Shanghai

Maiden of Orleans
A Bayou Thriller

Copyright © 2005 by Joseph Patrick Rogers

iUniverse books may be ordered through booksellers or by contacting:

iUniverse
2021 Pine Lake Road, Suite 100
Lincoln, NE 68512
www.iuniverse.com
1-800-Authors (1-800-288-4677)

ISBN-13: 978-0-595-36291-2 (pbk)
ISBN-13: 978-0-595-81709-2 (cloth)
ISBN-13: 978-0-595-80731-4 (ebk)
ISBN-10: 0-595-36291-5 (pbk)
ISBN-10: 0-595-81709-2 (cloth)
ISBN-10: 0-595-80731-3 (ebk)

Printed in the United States of America

CHAPTER 1

▼

"Dangers unimaginable lurk in the Bayou swamps," Jacqueline Faire told her two wide-eyed daughters seated next to her on the sofa. "I have lived in the Bayou for many years, girls, and I have heard many stories. I'm sure that some of these stories are tall tales, but some of them might be true."

"Are there werewolves in the swamps, Momma?" asked nine-year-old Lysette.

"There are, and one of them is going to climb through your window tonight and gobble you up!" declared twelve-year-old Lori, her face alight with gleeful mischief.

Pierre Faire looked up from the newspaper that he was reading in his chair across the room. "Lori, don't frighten your little sister."

"Yes, Poppa."

"I don't know about whether there are any werewolves hereabouts," Jacqueline said. "However, I did hear a tale about some pirates."

"Yay, pirates!" Lysette cheered, her fears about werewolves forgotten.

"Almost two hundred years ago a United States Navy ship chased a pirate ship along the Gulf Coast. For almost a day the Navy ship pursued the pirates along the southern edge of Louisiana. Then, in an attempt to escape from the Navy ship, the pirate ship left the open sea and turned into an inlet that flowed through the Bayou. The Navy ship pursued them, but the water soon became too shallow to sail in, and both ships became mired in the mud of the inland waterway."

"I'll bet that there was a big battle!" Lori loved adventure stories.

"Indeed, there was," Jacqueline resumed. "A fierce battle ensued. Both ships fired their cannons from point-blank range. When the ships were torn to shreds, the pirates and Navy crewmen charged at each other in the swamp. In waist-high water they fought with swords and guns. The two sides were so equally matched that eventually every man from both crews was killed."

When the two girls gasped, their mother concluded, "Now some folk today claim that the ghosts of these pirates and Navy crewmen still haunt the Bayou swamp. The need for a final, decisive victory by one side or the other prevents their spirits from achieving the peace necessary to move on to the next world. Since I've never seen any ghosts myself, I can't say whether or not this is a tall tale."

"I think that it really happened, and that there are lots of ghosts around here!" Lysette exclaimed.

"You could be correct, dear," Jacqueline said. "And now, whether there be ghosts or no, Lysette and Lori to bed shall go!"

After a brief, half-hearted protest, the girls went to their bedroom.

Pierre looked up over the top of his glasses at his wife. "Jacqueline, I assume that your intent was not to scare the girls so much that they won't be able to sleep until they are thirty years old. So exactly what was the purpose of that story?"

"I sometimes worry about the girls wandering out of the yard and going into the forest or down near the swamp," Jacqueline said. "Perhaps a few scary stories will keep them in our yard and out of trouble."

Pierre grinned. "With those two scamps that story is more likely to send them into the swamp searching for the wreck of that pirate ship."

"I didn't consider that possibility," she said with a smile.

"Well, don't worry about them. The only dangerous creatures that I know of in the Bayou are poisonous snakes and alligators, and the girls know to stay away from them. I'll be surprised if they encounter any ghosts or ghoulies or long-legged beasties or things that go bump in the night."

Jacqueline laughed. "So will I. In fact, the only thing around here that makes me nervous is the family that you work for in the big house on the hill."

"Now, Jacqueline, be kind. I've worked as a groundskeeper for almost twenty years for them. Everyone in the family has always treated me with respect. Mr. Claude Rasten has never said a harsh word to me, and he provides us with this nice cottage and decent wages."

"My friends at church tell me that there are rumors that they made their fortune by smuggling illegal drugs. And people say that most of the local politicians and judges are on the family payroll."

"Some persons are jealous of wealthy families like the Rastens," Pierre said. "We shouldn't listen to rumormongers. Many good persons have had their reputations damaged by false rumors."

"I have nothing against Mr. Claude Rasten. His son, Henri, gives me the creeps, though. Even though you don't like rumors, I'm going to tell you one more: Linda Thompson says that her nineteen-year-old daughter and some college friends saw Henri at a voodoo ceremony."

"A lot of folk in this region are interested in voodoo. That doesn't mean that they're bad persons."

"Dabbling with the occult can be dangerous."

"Yes dear. Let's hope that young Henri has satisfied his curiosity and won't venture into darker areas."

"That boy will seek out the darkest area that he can find," Jacqueline said. "You mark my words, Pierre."

"Yes, dear." Pierre returned his attention to his newspaper.

CHAPTER 2

▼

Seven years later Lori Faire walked down the dusty trail of a wooded hillside. Two small children skipped alongside her. Lori was now nineteen-years-old. Early in her teenage years, her hair color had become a light brown, while her younger sister, Lysette, remained blonde like their mother. All three had deep, rich brown eyes.

Lori worked part-time at the charter school from which she had graduated one year ago. The charter school, which had been established by some local residents, included students from kindergarten through high school. Usually two or three grades were combined in a single classroom.

In the morning Lori served as a teacher's assistant for the kindergarten and first grade pupils. In the afternoon she was allowed to use the distance learning classroom in order to take college classes using the Internet and a video link.

Lori hoped someday to attend Loyola University of New Orleans or some other Louisiana college, but for the present, this long-distance method of earning college credit seemed to be her only option. She planned to study art and astronomy, although she was uncertain which would be her major and which would be her minor.

When school was over in the afternoon, she walked home the six-year-old twin sisters, Katie and Kristin. The twins lived in a small house on the Rasten estate; their father had been employed as the groundskeeper since Lori's father had died.

Lori enjoyed the company of the bouncy, good-natured twins. Sometimes she would babysit them on the weekend. She liked to tell them stories, but she always omitted stories that might frighten them.

Lori and the twins were allowed to use the swimming pool at the mansion. They often explored the woods; Lori would take the girls to the best spots that she and Lysette had discovered in earlier years.

They found the circular, stone table and bench where they suspected gnomes and wood sprites held midnight feasts. They waded under a waterfall that seemed to flow out of fairyland.

Lori could not take the girls too far, though, because Lori did not know how to drive and her family did not have a car. As a result of watching television and reading books, she knew that her isolated lifestyle in the Bayou was unusual for a nineteen-year-old girl.

She sometimes wondered whether her family's isolation was merely the result of chance circumstances or whether they had been isolated for a reason. Yet Lori knew that there was danger in the large world outside their Bayou community, and until recently, she had felt safe and protected within the boundaries of her small world.

As they neared the twins' cottage, Lori turned around and looked back along the trail. "Did you see something moving back there?"

"Maybe it's a deer," Katie suggested, peering back into the trees.

"Ha! I'll bet that it's a big monster!" Kristin exclaimed gleefully. "It will probably grab us and take us back to its cave."

Lori laughed. "Most likely it's my imagination."

Once she saw the girls safely into their cottage, Lori resumed her trek along the trail that led to her own cottage. She continued to feel like she was being followed, but whenever she glanced back, there was nothing and no one there.

Her feelings of unease increased as she moved through a heavily-wooded area near the Rasten mansion. Lori quickened her pace; she felt especially vulnerable amongst the dark shadows cast by the trees.

In spite of the unevenness of the trail, Lori decided to risk running the rest of the way home. However, just as she was about to begin jogging, one of the shadows up ahead seemed to solidify into human form and a man strode forward toward her.

Lori blinked and looked again, realizing that the interplay of sunlight and shadow had deceived her eyes. It was now clear that what she had seen was merely Oliver Paisley walking out of the shade of the trees.

Oliver was a tall, dark-haired man in his late twenties. He was the executive assistant of Henri Rasten, the man who now ruled the Rasten financial empire. Lori supposed that Oliver was rather handsome, but there was something mysterious and dangerous about him. This aura of mystery would be appealing to some women; however, Lori did not like the man.

"Good afternoon, Miss Faire. I'm sorry if I startled you," Paisley said upon seeing her reaction.

"That's quite all right, Mr. Paisley," she said, regaining her poise. "I seem to be a bit jumpy today."

"I was sitting out on the veranda when I noticed you coming down the trail," Oliver said. "Mr. Rasten asked me to find you and escort you to the mansion. He is anxious to speak with you."

Lori suppressed a sigh. She knew the matter about which Henri wanted to speak with her. Lori had hoped that the matter would simply go away, that Henri would become involved with a woman in his own social circle and forget about her.

"I have a lot of homework to do for my college classes, Mr. Paisley. I'd rather speak with Mr. Rasten tomorrow afternoon. Please convey my apologies."

Oliver remained standing in her path, and he gave no indication that he planned to move.

"Mr. Rasten was very insistent that I bring you to see him. He will be angry with both of us if you don't come with me."

"All right," she agreed reluctantly. She was afraid that if she refused, Oliver would physically force her to accompany him. Lori had always maintained a civil relationship with the man, and she preferred that things continue that way.

They did not converse as she trudged along the trail behind him. After a short distance, they walked out of the woods, across a well-kept lawn, and onto the veranda. He held the patio door open for Lori and entered the mansion behind her.

"Mr. Rasten is waiting for you in his study." Oliver watched her walk down the hallway and knock on the study door, then he went away to handle some other unknown duty.

"Come in," Henri's voice came from the office in response to Lori's knock.

As she opened the door and entered the room, he rose from the chair and approached her. Henri was in his mid-thirties and was similar in appearance to Oliver, except Henri was an inch shorter.

"Hello, Lori." When he kissed her on the cheek, he noticed that her body became tense, almost rigid.

"Hi, Mr. Rasten." Lori relaxed slightly when he took a step backwards.

"I thought that we were on a first name basis."

"Yes, Henri."

"That sounds much better. I guess that you know why I wanted to speak with you today."

"Yes, but I have not changed my mind. I do not want to marry anyone for quite a while."

"I think that I have been patient with you, but I am not willing to delay any longer," Henri said. "We must plan our wedding. I can abide no further delay."

"I have no intention of marrying you, sir."

He sighed. "We have had this discussion previously, Lori. As you know, when you were seventeen years old, your father made a commitment that you would marry me when you turned eighteen. Your father and I signed legal documents formalizing that commitment."

"He is dead," she said flatly.

"Yes, it was a most unfortunate accident. However, his death does not negate the contract. You are still obliged to marry me."

"I do not love you, sir."

"You will learn to love me eventually. You are a schoolgirl with little knowledge of the real world. I could have insisted that you marry me on your eighteenth birthday. Because of your reluctance, though, I have patiently waited for over a year. You are now nineteen years old and still do not want to honor a contract. You repay my generosity with childish petulance."

"If I am so childish, you should ignore me for a few years until I am more mature."

He laughed. "Oh, I find your petulance to be one of your beguiling qualities." Henri stared at her. "Our marriage must occur very soon for reasons that you would not understand. I am going to arrange for our wedding to be held one week from Saturday."

Lori was shocked. "I will not be there," she said, taking a couple of steps away from him.

"Of course, you will. And I expect you to be in attendance at my Halloween masquerade this weekend. We can announce our engagement at the party."

"I refuse to marry you!"

"You will do what you are told! Oliver is going to go to your cottage and pack up your possessions to bring here. We have prepared a room for you upstairs. You will be living in this mansion from now on."

Lori became frantic. "I want to go home!" she shouted.

"This is your home now."

"It is not!"

Lori bolted out of the study and down the hallway. She flung open the front door and ran off the porch and across the lawn toward the woods.

"What is going on, sir?" a startled maid asked Henri as he emerged from the study.

"Nothing that concerns you," he replied curtly. "Where is Oliver?"

"Here I am." Oliver was hurrying toward the front door. "I saw the girl. Do you want me to go after her?"

"Yes, but I don't see any need to engage in a footrace with her. I would expect that Lori is merely running home to her mother. Take two men down to their cottage, see to it that she packs some clothing, and bring her back here."

While Oliver went to get two of his men, Henri returned to the study and looked out the picture window toward the woods. I am cursed with an obsession for that girl, he reflected. It distracts me from my fixed purpose. How did I allow myself to be placed in a position where my entire future depends upon her? What dark spirit has seized my soul?

CHAPTER 3

—————————— ▼ ——————————

Lori raced through the woods with a wild abandon. She knew that she had to escape, but she did not know where she was going. Henri had misjudged her predictability; in spite of her panic, Lori had quickly decided that she would not return home because she knew that they would come looking for her there. She did not want to endanger her mother and sister, both of whom Lori knew would resist her abduction.

Lori headed in the direction of the swamp. She reasoned that she knew the swamp better than anyone, certainly better than any of Henri's hired thugs, so she would have the best chance of eluding pursuers there.

The ground gradually sloped downward as she moved deep into the woods. Soon Lori found herself running through ankle-deep water.

A feeling of being watched came upon her. Lori glanced back and, for a moment, thought that she saw someone moving through the trees. Lori stopped running and intently scanned the area, but there did not seem to be anyone there.

She wondered whether the same phantom that she had sensed following her earlier on the trail with the children was in pursuit of her now. *My imagination seems to be running even faster than I am,* she thought.

Lori went splashing into knee-high water. She spotted an alligator gliding stealthily through some underbrush. This did not frighten Lori, though, because through the years she and Lysette had encountered many alligators in the swamps and none of them had bothered Lori and Lysette. It had almost seemed to Lori that there was an implied peace treaty between the alligators and the girls. In fact, no animal in the woods or in the swamp had ever threatened either girl.

Upon reaching a familiar tree, Lori paused to catch her breath. From a common trunk, three smaller trunks branched off in different directions forming a comfortable nook up into which Lori boosted herself. She needed to sit and think.

Where am I going? I can only hide in this swamp for a day or two. I have five dollars and twenty-five cents in my pocket. She began to despair. *I can't go back to school; everyone would be gone by now, and the building would be locked. Besides, in order to get there, I'd need to go back past the Rasten estate. They'd probably catch me. I can't go to the twins' house; that will probably be one of the first places that they search for me.* Then an idea popped into her mind, and hope was renewed as a plan started to take shape.

Oliver Paisley and two of his men slowly approached the cottage where the Faire family lived.

"Wait back here in the trees," he told the two men. "You might not be needed."

Oliver walked across the clearing and knocked on the front door. Jacqueline Faire opened the door almost immediately. A look of surprise flashed across her face when she recognized her visitor.

"Mr. Paisley, good afternoon."

"Hello, Mrs. Faire. I would like to speak to Lori."

"So would I!" Jacqueline declared. "That girl is almost two hours late getting home from school. I'm becoming worried about her." She glanced at Oliver, suspicion showing in her eyes. "Why do you want to see Lori?"

"On her way home from school, I happened to run into Lori. I mentioned to her that Mr. Rasten wanted to see her, and she graciously agreed to speak with him at the mansion. However, she became upset when he mentioned their engagement, and she ran off. Mr. Rasten is concerned about her and sent me to make certain that she is all right."

"Henri Rasten needs to forget about that so-called engagement," Jacqueline said. "Lori is not going to marry him. She won't be ready to marry anyone for a long time."

"Well, they'll need to work that matter out between themselves. Good-bye, Mrs. Faire. Please let us know when Lori returns home." Oliver turned around and walked away.

Jacqueline watched him for a few seconds, then shut the door. She immediately went to the telephone and called the twins' cottage. Jacqueline quickly explained the situation to the twins' mother.

"I haven't seen Lori since she brought the girls home, Mrs. Faire. Lori looked to be in good spirits then, although the girls mentioned later that Lori thought that someone was following them."

"I'm very worried about her," Jacqueline said.

"I'll call you right away if we hear from Lori. I should tell you that over the last few weeks, my husband has become increasingly concerned about some things that he has seen going on. I don't want to go into details on the telephone. After discussing the situation, we decided that we should move somewhere that we'd feel more comfortable raising the twins. My husband has found a new job in New Orleans, and we'll be moving next week."

"We'll all miss you and your family. Lori and Lysette are so fond of the twins."

"We'll arrange for you and your girls to come visit us. Please let me know when Lori gets safely home."

"I will," Jacqueline promised.

After concluding her phone conversation, Jacqueline went to sit on the sofa, lost in thought. Lysette approached her mother.

"I'll bet that Lori is hiding in the swamp," Lysette said with confidence. "I know all of her favorite spots. Do you want me to go look for her?"

"No, dear. Then I would have to worry about both of you. Let's wait here for another hour. If she's not home by then, I'll go with you into the swamp. I agree with you that she probably went there. I wish that you girls didn't like that swamp so much."

At that moment, back in the swamp, Lori was about to put her plan into action. She climbed out of her resting spot in the tree and lowered herself into the water.

Looking toward the southeast, she moved into deeper water that came up to her waist. Lori had recalled that the Rastens had a boathouse nearby. It was close to where the swamp merged into an inlet that flowed out of the Gulf of Mexico.

Lori had been to the boathouse once when the estate's maintenance man had taken Lori and Lysette for jet ski rides. She remembered that it had been great fun to go cruising out of the inland waterway and onto the Gulf waters.

On that occasion, in order to reach the boathouse, they had ridden in the man's truck along the gravel road that extended from the rear of the mansion over high, dry ground to the inlet.

I guess that I'm taking the scenic route today, Lori thought wryly as she slogged her way toward her destination. Once I get in the boathouse I can take either a jet ski or a powerboat, then ride it to New Orleans. I should be able to sell it for at least two thousand dollars. That will give me enough money to live on for a while. I can rent an apartment and get a job. Then I can figure out a way to bring Momma and Lysette to the city.

Lori was not certain whether her plan was a good one and knew that many things could go awry, but having a definite course of action to follow made her feel better. She was not a hysterical girl; she was a young woman who had devised a plan that could succeed.

A hooting owl reminded Lori that evening was fast approaching and that she should not delay; she wanted to be onto the Gulf of Mexico before dark.

Lori felt like a special forces commando as she moved stealthily through the water near the boathouse. She was aware that there might be a workman on duty there, and she could not allow him to see her. Recalling how the alligators blended in harmoniously with their environment, Lori tried to do likewise.

She saw no one around. Lori emerged from the water and walked alongside the wooden wall of the boathouse. She peeked through a window. There was no one inside.

As Lori moved toward the door, she spotted the workman; the young man and his girlfriend were drinking beers on a bench about fifty yards away. Neither of them was looking in her direction.

Lori turned the doorknob, jumped inside, and quickly shut the door. She breathed a sigh of relief that the door had not been locked.

Her eyes surveyed the room. There were two speedboats and eight jet skis. Lori almost immediately dismissed the idea of taking one of the powerboats; they looked like they would be difficult to maneuver out of the crowded boathouse, and she was uncertain about how to operate a speedboat.

Lori went over to a jet ski that appeared similar to the one on which she had ridden. She experienced a sinking feeling when she remembered that she needed a lanyard key in order to start its engine. There was no lanyard on the watercraft. Neither of the jet skis next to it had lanyards either.

Lori ran over to search the desk. There were no lanyards on the desktop and the drawers were locked.

She began to experience feelings of panic again. Her plan seemed to be coming apart. Then she spotted a wooden rack on the wall; the lanyards were hanging from pegs. She grabbed a handful of lanyards and hurried back to the jet skis.

Just as she was about to sit down on one of the watercraft, she noticed that its fuel gauge indicated that it was almost out of gas. She leaned over and read the gauge on the adjacent jet ski: it was completely out of fuel.

Lori silently grumbled about that lazy workman. He should have been spending the afternoon getting these watercraft ready for use.

Instead of doing his work, he sits around drinking beer with some girl.

After examining several more fuel gauges, she found a jet ski with an almost full tank. Lori sighed with relief. She pushed the jet ski onto the cement ramp that sloped down into the water.

Lori tried to be quiet as she raised the waterside door, which rolled upward like a garage door. As soon as she got the craft into the water, Lori climbed onto the large, cushioned seat.

She inserted the lanyard key, pushed the start button, and went roaring out of the boathouse. It was impossible to sneak away on one of these vehicles.

Lori looked back over her shoulder to see the young workman running toward the water. She did not know him, and she could not hear what he was shouting. He would never catch her.

A joyful feeling of empowerment came over her as she accelerated through the inland waterway and sped toward the Gulf of Mexico.

CHAPTER 4

▼

Henri Rasten tapped his foot impatiently as he sat in his office and waited for news. Oliver Paisley walked through the open doorway.

"Did you find her?" Henri asked.

"Not yet. I went to her house, but she hadn't returned home yet. I posted one of my men in the woods near the cottage so that he can intercept her if she goes back there. The girl sometimes babysits for the groundskeeper's children. Just a few minutes ago I checked at that house, but Lori was not there either. I suppose that she might be hiding in the swamp. I can take some men down there to begin a search. There are so many square miles of area to search, though; I'm guessing that we won't catch her until she gets hungry and thirsty and goes home."

"I've activated the phone tap on her home telephone," Henri said. "I suppose that I should also activate the tap on the groundskeeper's home phone in case she calls his family."

"This girl is an awful lot of trouble," Oliver said. "She is beautiful, but there are many beautiful women in Louisiana. You are considered the most eligible bachelor in this region. Why don't you just forget about this girl and select a different fiancee?"

"You know that I am not marrying her merely because of her beauty. I have to marry her. For the past two years at our rituals, the spirit guides have told me that if I do not marry Lori Faire, I will perish." Henri picked up a stack of Tarot cards that he always kept on his desk. With a fanning motion, he spread them across the desktop. "Even these damned cards indicate that I am damned if I don't marry that damned girl."

Oliver laughed. "Then we had better find her. However, I know from past experience that messages from spirit guides are often ambiguous. They seldom tell us everything. If they tell you that you will meet with misfortune if you do not marry Lori Faire, perhaps they neglect to tell you that you will meet with worse misfortune if you do marry her."

"Thank you so much for that encouraging message," Henri said sarcastically. "You are more experienced with the occult than I am, Oliver, however, I do know that the words of spirit guides can be interpreted in more than one way."

Oliver shrugged. "Well, she's a feisty girl, but I suppose that you'll be able to control her."

Henri nodded. "I have spells that will break the girl's willfulness. Within a year, she'll be the most docile wife in the Bayou."

Oliver's cell phone rang. He answered the call and listened for about twenty seconds.

"All right. We'll need to go after her. Get a speedboat and several jet skis ready to go. I'll be down at the boathouse with several men in a few minutes." He hung up.

"What has happened?" Henri asked anxiously.

"Your docile bride-to-be just stole one of your jet skis and is headed for the high seas."

Henri smiled ruefully. "I might need more than a year to break that one's spirit."

Lori was having difficulty controlling the jet ski. She had managed to navigate her way through the inlet and out onto the Gulf coastal waters. However, she had cut her turns too sharply on two occasions and nearly capsized. Now, as she coasted along the shallow water near the beach, she was having difficulty adjusting to the waves.

On her only other jet ski ride, Lori had been a passenger most of the time. When their family's friend had allowed her to "take the helm" for a few minutes, he had been seated directly behind her and had helped her control the jet ski.

In spite of her difficulties, Lori felt like she was beginning to gain the feel of handling it. She gradually headed out into deeper water.

Sunset had begun, and some boats returned to port. With her range of vision, Lori could see two sailboats, three jet skis, a powerboat moving fast, and a fishing boat going quite slowly as its passengers tried to make a big catch.

Lori's eyes continually returned to the larger of the two sailboats. It was about forty feet long and had multi-colored sails with blue and gold being the principal colors.

Hearing the distant hum of engines, Lori shifted her gaze back in the direction from which she had come. To her horror, a speedboat and five jet skis had emerged from the inlet about a mile away from her present location. She had no doubt that the craft were piloted by men pursuing her.

Fortunately, Lori had seen them first. She steered her own watercraft to the starboard side of the large sailboat that she had been admiring. Its high, billowing sails effectively screened her from the view of Henri's men.

In addition, the sailboat was heading away from the inlet. Lori adjusted her course to stay parallel to the boat. She could see its captain at the helm; he was watching her as he moved the wheel slightly to maintain his course.

Lori looked back to see that some of Henri's men had gone out into deeper water in order to check on the identity of a young woman on one of the other jet skis.

As soon as they realize that she is not the person for whom they are searching, they'll look in this direction and spot me, she thought as feelings of panic returned. I'm no longer screened from their view!

Lori considered increasing to maximum speed and making an all-out run away from her pursuers. She quickly rejected that idea, though; the speedboat would likely catch her within two or three miles.

Instead, she decided to maneuver around to the port side of the sailboat and try to continue to use it as a screen. Lori sped up to move ahead of the boat. However, in her haste, she repeated her earlier mistakes: she cut too sharply left and failed to adjust for a large wave. The jet ski capsized, and Lori went somersaulting over the handlebars and under the water. For a couple of seconds, she was unsure which way was up and which way was down, but then she managed to find her way to the surface.

Lori flayed her arms wildly as she attempted to grab hold of the jet ski that she was certain must be floating nearby. Another wave hit her and she swallowed some salt water.

Where is that jet ski? She recalled that there had been several life-preservers on a wall rack in the boathouse. I should have taken one, Lori reprimanded herself. I barely know how to swim.

Lori looked up at the sailboat. It seemed to have stopped, and the captain was looking over the railing at her.

A third wave knocked her underwater again. After a few seconds of intense effort, she managed to struggle to the surface, gasping for breath. Lori gazed upward to the spot at the boat's railing where the man had been standing. He was no longer there.

In a moment of utter desperation, Lori felt that she had been abandoned. He must have gone into his boat's cabin so that he wouldn't have to watch me die, she thought with despair as a wave took her underwater yet again.

Lysette and Momma will miss me so much, and I'll miss them. And I did so want to go to a real college.

Lori sank into the Gulf of Mexico, knowing that she would never surface again by her own power.

Then, suddenly, something large and heavy collided into her. Lori's first thought was that it was a shark. Can't it wait for me to drown before it eats me?

When she felt an arm wrap around her waist, she had a second and more accurate thought: the man did not go into his sailboat's cabin; he was no longer standing at the railing because he had jumped into the water and was swimming towards me.

The man swam to the surface, cradling Lori against him She gulped in some air, then lost consciousness for a few seconds.

As she awoke, he was carrying her up the rope ladder that hung along the hull of his boat. He held Lori tightly against his body as though he had found the sea's most precious treasure.

CHAPTER 5

▼

The man laid her gently on the deck and began to give her mouth-to-mouth resuscitation. Lori spat out some of the salt water that she had swallowed. Soon she began to revive and feel better. Lori opened one eye in order to get a surreptitious look at the man who was continuing to resuscitate her. He appeared to be about thirty years old and was better-than-average looking with sandy brown hair and sea green eyes.

Upon noticing that her eyes were open, the man stopped his ministrations and raised himself to one knee.

"Well, hello there. You had me worried for a while. How are you feeling?"

"Much better, thank you," Lori answered shyly. She felt comfortable resting on the deck and talking to this man. "You have a very pretty sailboat."

"Thank you, although I hope that my boat didn't cause you to become distracted and lose control of your jet ski."

Lori jumped as if jolted by an electrical charge. She remembered what had caused her to capsize.

"What's wrong?" The man thought that she was having a seizure.

"I'm still in danger," Lori said and raised herself to her knees in order to peek over the side of the boat. "Those men on jet skis and in the speedboat are searching for me."

"Why?'

"It's quite a long story. I'll tell you later. Right now, I need to hide."

"Go down into the cabin. I'll get rid of the men."

"Okay." Keeping low, she hurried over to the steps and descended into the cabin.

The man considered turning on his boat's engine so that they could get out of the area faster, but he did not want to do anything that might attract the attention of the pursuers.

Two of the jet skis were within a quarter-mile of his boat. The man knew that he and his passenger had been fortunate that no pursuers had yet come to investigate why a sailboat had stopped for almost seven minutes.

Not wanting to press his luck any further, he tried to get the boat moving again as quickly as possible. He turned the wheel so that the boat was no longer pointing directly into the wind. Gradually, the mainsail and jib filled with wind, and the boat began to pick up speed.

The man glanced to starboard to see two jet skis closing in. He returned his attention to the water directly ahead, ignoring the jet skis.

"Hey!" one of the riders shouted to him.

He looked over at them. "Can I help you?"

"Yeah, we're looking for a girl on a jet ski. Have you seen her?"

The man pointed off in the distance behind them. "I did notice a young lady who seemed to be having difficulty controlling her jet ski a couple of miles back. She might have capsized. Would you like for me to call the Coast Guard on my radio?"

"No, that's okay," the rider answered quickly. "We'll make sure that she's all right."

The two jet skis went speeding away. In a short while they were almost out of sight.

For the next few minutes the man concentrated on trimming his sails for maximum efficiency. Then he noticed two wide eyes gazing up at him from the shadows on the cabin steps.

"It's safe to come up now," the man assured Lori. "Your pursuers are many miles away by now."

"Good." She came onto the deck and sat down on the cushioned bench along the stern rail.

"What is your name?" the man asked.

"Lori Faire."

"My name is Mikhail Xavier." He reached out to shake hands with her.

Lori found it amusing to be exchanging a casual handshake with someone whose lips had been pressed against hers only a short while earlier. Not wanting Mikhail to think that she was immature, she resisted the urge to giggle.

Then she remembered something that instantly dispelled her feelings of levity.

"My jet ski!" she cried, looking toward the water. "Were you able to recover it?"

"No, when you capsized, the waves pushed it underwater," he replied, surprised by her sudden change of mood.

"But I thought that jet skis were designed to float when they turned over."

"They are, but while we were in the water, I lost track of it, and apparently the waves carried it away. The jet ski should wash up on the beach. I could come back tomorrow and look for it. Do you have any insurance on your jet ski?"

"It's not actually mine. I took it from Henri Rasten's boathouse in order to escape from his estate." Seeing Mikhail's amused expression, she became more exasperated. "You consider it funny because I'm upset about losing a jet ski that I stole. But you don't understand! Losing it messes up my entire plan! I was going to try to sell it for two thousand dollars." She fought back her tears. "I planned to live off that money until I could rescue my mother and sister." She pulled a soggy five-dollar bill out of the pocket of her jeans. "This is all the money that I have." She gave it to Mikhail. "I want to pay you for giving me a ride on your boat."

Mikhail handed the money back to her. "You happened to come aboard on free ride day." He moved toward the stairs. "I need to get something from the cabin. I'll be right back."

Lori watched him go down into the cabin. I am completely within the power of this man, and I don't know anything about him, Lori reflected. He is obviously wealthy. He seems to find me attractive. Perhaps, like the old saying warns, I've gone from the frying pan into the fire.

As Mikhail came back up the steps, Lori asked him bluntly, "Are you a friend of Henri Rasten?"

He laughed. "I never know what you are going to say next. In answer to your question, I am not his friend. I know Henri Rasten, but I do not like him."

"That's good because I don't like him either," Lori said.

Mikhail gave her an envelope stuffed with money. "Here's five hundred dollars." Guessing what she was thinking, he added, "There are no strings attached. This is an unconditional gift."

"I intend to pay you back sometime after I find a job," Lori insisted.

"That will be fine."

Mikhail had also brought up from the cabin some soda cans and snacks. He and Lori sat down on the cushioned bench along the stern rail. From where he was seated, Mikhail could reach the wheel in order to make small corrections to the boat's course.

"I'm sorry that I got so fussy about losing the jet ski," Lori said after taking a few drinks from the cold Dr. Pepper can. "I'm not usually so crabby, but I've had a very difficult day. You've only seen my most recent ordeals." Lori proceeded to tell him everything that had happened since she left the charter school that afternoon.

Mikhail listened with rapt attention. He marveled at this young woman's strength and ingenuity.

"So here I am," she concluded her tale, flashing a winning grin at Mikhail.

"And I'm very happy that you are here," Mikhail said warmly. "I'll forever be able to tell the story about the evening that I pulled a lovely mermaid from the sea."

Lori's grin widened. "If I were a mermaid, I'd be a much better swimmer."

"I'm not a good swimmer either," Mikhail said.

"That makes your act of jumping into the water to save me even more heroic; you could have drowned, too," Lori said and added with a wink, "I'll try not to fall overboard so that you don't have to rescue me again."

Mikhail laughed. "Thanks. I guess we've both had enough swimming practice for one evening."

CHAPTER 6

▼

Perched comfortably on the cushioned bench, Lori watched with admiration Mikhail's skillful handling of his vessel.

"You are a great sailor." She looked up at the stars that had begun appearing in the evening sky. It was now almost completely dark. Lori pointed upward. "There's the North Star. Sailors throughout history have used it to find their way home. I can identify a lot of the constellations, and I plan to study astronomy in college."

"I'd like to learn celestial navigation someday," Mikhail said. "At the present for long trips I need to rely on my electronic equipment that links with global positioning satellites to give me my longitude and latitude coordinates. If my satellite link goes down, I don't know where the heck I am. I should hire you to be my navigator."

"First I have to learn more about celestial navigation," Lori said with a giggle.

"I'll leave the job open for you until you're ready."

Mikhail got up and made some adjustments to the trim of the sails.

"Would you like to take the helm for a while?" he asked.

"Can I?" Lori was excited.

"Sure. Just take hold of the wheel." He pointed at a tower on the distant shore. "Aim the boat at that tower. You'll frequently need to make small course corrections because the wind and water movement tend to push you off course."

For about ten minutes Lori relished the experience of sailing the large, attractive ship. Mikhail was glad to see her so happy.

"We're getting close to the marina, Lori. I'd better take the wheel now."

"Okay. That was great. Thanks a lot."

Mikhail turned on the engine and guided the boat into a brightly-illuminated wharf. He deftly maneuvered into a berth that was reserved for his sailboat. After securing the docking lines, he returned his attention to Lori.

"I have some shrimp in the cabin's refrigerator. I'll heat them up in the microwave for our dinner."

"That sounds good," Lori said. "While you're preparing dinner, I'd like to call my mother. She must be terribly worried about me."

Mikhail got his cellular phone from the cabin, then went back down while Lori made her call.

Meanwhile, back at her family's cottage, Jacqueline and Lysette had just returned from their search of the swamp.

"You have to believe me, Momma!" Lysette insisted. "Close to where the water gets deeper I saw a man in a white Navy uniform. He looked straight at me, then pointed out toward the inlet. I think that he was trying to tell me that Lori went in that direction. Lori is heading toward the Gulf beaches!"

"I don't have time to listen to ghost stories," Jacqueline said, tired and discouraged. "I should never have filled your head with those fanciful tales. Your sister is missing, and I need to decide what to do next. I'm beginning to suspect that she's being kept against her will up at the mansion. That visit by Oliver Paisley might have been for the purpose of fooling us into thinking that he and Henri Rasten don't know where Lori is." Jacqueline looked intently at Lysette. "You mark my words, girl: there's evil afoot in that Rasten mansion!"

At that second the telephone rang, startling both of them.

"Hello?" Jacqueline answered.

"Momma, it's me."

"Lori!" she exclaimed. "Thank God. Are you all right?"

"I'm fine. After school today, Henri Rasten demanded that I marry him next week! He was going to keep me confined at his house, but I ran away! I took a jet ski from the boathouse, and I escaped" Lori paused, then as if guided by a sixth sense or some intuition of danger, she became more cautious in what she revealed. "I had some difficulty with the jet ski, but I made it to the Gulf of Mexico, and I have found a safe place to stay."

Just as Jacqueline was about to ask for more details, she guessed the reason for Lori's reticence.

"Perhaps I'd better not keep you on the phone any longer since phone calls can be traced," Jacqueline said.

"Yes, Momma. I just wanted to tell you that you don't need to worry about me. I'm about to have a hot meal. And I have plenty of money."

"Your guardian angel must be looking out for you, dear. Call me again soon."

"I will, Momma," Lori promised. "Bye."

After Jacqueline hung up, she felt tension flow out of her body. For the first time in several hours she could relax a little.

"What did she say? What did she say?" Lysette was bouncing with curiosity.

Jacqueline repeated what Lori had told her.

"So I was right! The ghost of the Navy officer showed me where Lori had gone." Lysette was delighted by her vindication.

"Were you able to set your mother's mind at ease?" Mikhail asked Lori as she sat down at the cabin table.

"Yep. Now she'll be able to sleep tonight."

"Good."

Mikhail had prepared a simple meal that consisted of shrimp, Italian vegetable soup with crackers, and Pepsi colas. As he placed the meal before her, Lori looked intently at his hands.

"When you shook hands with me earlier, you were careful to shake my hand gently, but I could tell that you have strong hands," Lori said. She had little experience around men and wondered whether Mikhail's strength was far above average.

"I play golf fairly often; that probably develops my hand muscles. And I have studied fencing for several years. You're supposed to control your sword primarily with the thumb and forefingers. That also helps to build strong hands. I'm fairly ambidextrous, and I sometimes fence left-handed and sometimes right-handed."

"I've seen fencing on television; it looks like great fun," Lori said. "However, my favorite sport to watch is figure skating. Someday I'd like to take ice skating lessons. My sister and I have done some rollerblading, but we've never skated on ice."

"Well, one of these days, we'll go in search of an ice rink."

At the conclusion of their dinner, Lori and Mikhail cleared the table.

"I'd recommend that you spend the night on this boat, Lori," Mikhail said and added hastily, "I'm going to go home to my condominium. You'll have the sailboat all to yourself. There's a nice sleeping berth over there with pillows and a blanket. After I leave, you can lock the cabin doors from the inside. You'll be safe here."

"You're so kind to me, Mikhail." Lori's eyes misted with tears.

"I'm always glad to be of service to a damsel in distress." Mikhail picked up a notepad and wrote his home phone number. "I'll leave my cell phone with you tonight. Call me if you feel afraid. There's a night manager on duty at this marina. His name is Tomas Nyssa. He's a good man, and he makes several patrols every night. You'll probably hear him walking along the docks. Occasionally, boats come in overnight that are returning from a cruise or that want to purchase fuel, so don't worry if you hear a boat's engines."

"Don't worry about me. I'll be fine, Mikhail. When will you be back?"

He moved onto the cabin steps. "I'll try to get here by ten o'clock tomorrow morning. Sleep well, Lori Faire."

"I shall, thanks to you, Mikhail Xavier. Good-night."

Mikhail ascended the steps and walked out onto the deck where he paused long enough to hear Lori lock the cabin doors. He went across the docks to the marina office. Mikhail owned this marina whose main business was renting boats, jet skis, and kayaks.

The night manager, Tomas Nyssa, came forward to greet him. Tomas was a short, sturdily-built man in his mid-forties.

"How was sailing this evening, Mikhail?"

"It was fantastic, Tomas. This was my most enjoyable evening of sailing ever. During my voyage, I took aboard a passenger who will be staying aboard my boat tonight. This young lady could be in some danger, so I'd appreciate it if you could keep a close watch on my boat."

"Of course, Mikhail."

"Keep the gun ready and nearby, Tomas. I think that tonight should be quiet, but I expect trouble in the near future."

"You can count on us to stand with you against whatever comes against you, Mikhail."

"I know, Tomas. Thank you. Good-night."

CHAPTER 7

▼

At eight o'clock the next morning Oliver Paisley came into Henri Rasten's office.

"Good news," Henri told him. "My phone tap picked up a call from Lori to her mother last night." Henri proceeded to play the recording for Oliver.

"The girl was cautious about how much she revealed," Oliver remarked. "She didn't want to tell where she was staying."

Henri grinned. "Yes, isn't that remarkable? Lori suspected that we had a tap on the phone line. I seem to have underestimated her. Where could she be staying?"

"There were over two hundred persons along that stretch of Gulf beaches," Oliver said. "She might have befriended some college students and left with them. Or perhaps some family took pity upon the poor little waif and took her back to their house. In any case, I'm glad to hear that she's alive. I was afraid that she had drowned."

"So was I," Henri said. "How are we going to find her?

"I have the men checking at all the hotels and motels along a twelve-mile stretch of coast. It might take a couple of days to do a thorough job."

"I'm going to contact the Sheriff. He can arrange to trace the call the next time Lori calls her mother."

"That will probably be our best way to track her down," Oliver said. "In the meantime, I'm going to go on a scouting mission along the coast. Many of the recreational craft on the water yesterday evening were from the Xavier boat rental marina. In fact, we saw Mikhail Xavier himself out sailing his yacht. I think that I'll go to his marina and ask if any of his customers reported seeing the girl."

"Do you know Mikhail Xavier?" Henri asked.

"I met him once at a party given by Michelle Fournier. He probably would remember me."

"If he knows that you work for me, he won't tell you anything useful."

"As you know, I have my own methods of discerning the truth," Oliver said.

"Your gifts have served me well," Henri acknowledged.

A short while later Oliver was driving along the Gulf coast. He stopped by a couple of motels in order to show Lori's photograph to the desk clerks and to some guests standing nearby. No one had seen her.

At about ten o'clock in the morning he arrived at the Xavier boat rental marina. After parking on the lot, Oliver went into the office where the clerk was helping a customer. Without waiting, he passed through the office and emerged on the docks.

Oliver almost crashed into Mikhail Xavier, who was placing some coins into a soda machine. Mikhail glanced up, a look of surprise appearing momentarily on his face and quickly replaced by his usual calm demeanor.

"Mikhail, I'm Oliver Paisley," he said, extending his hand. "We met last year at Michelle Fournier's party."

Mikhail shook his hand. "Yes, of course, Oliver, I remember you. It's good to see you again. Would you like to rent a boat today?"

"I wish that I had the time. Today, however, I'm on an assignment for my employer, Henri Rasten."

"Oh, how can I help you?"

Oliver handed him the photograph of Lori. "This young lady is the daughter of a deceased employee of Mr. Rasten, who generously allows her family to continue to live on his estate. Unfortunately, the girl has severe emotional problems. She has run away from home. Mr. Rasten and the girl's family are very concerned about her well-being. Have you seen this girl?"

Mikhail looked intently at Lori's photograph. "I'm pretty sure that I saw her yesterday evening. When I was out sailing, I noticed a young woman who was having difficulty controlling her jet ski. She closely resembled the young lady in this picture." He returned the photograph to Oliver. "It appeared inevitable that she would eventually capsize. I hope that she didn't drown."

"Some of the jet skis and boats in that area last night were rentals from here. Did any of your customers mention seeing her?"

"No one said anything to me about her," Mikhail said. "I could check with some of my regular customers and the night manager. If I find out anything that you should know, I'll give you a call."

"All right."

Oliver was perplexed. For years he had possessed the power to determine the truthfulness of what a person told him. Yet Oliver could not sense either falsehood or truth in anything that was said by the man who stood before him. Mikhail Xavier seemed to be beyond Oliver's powers.

"Be sure to let me know when the young woman makes it safely back home," Mikhail said pleasantly, not at all bothered by the intense scrutiny of Oliver's dark eyes.

"I'll do that. Good-bye." Oliver turned and walked away. He did not like anyone whom he could not intimidate.

Mikhail watched him go through the office, out onto the parking lot, get in a car, and drive away. When Mikhail was convinced that Oliver was not going to double back, Mikhail walked over to his sailboat.

He stepped onto the deck. Just as he was about to knock on the cabin doors, they were flung open. Lori popped out like a jack-in-the-box.

"That was Oliver Paisley!" she exclaimed.

"And good morning to you, too, Miss Lori."

Mikhail's nonchalance helped to calm Lori.

"Good morning yourself. What did he want?"

"He's looking for my mermaid." Mikhail proceeded to retell his conversation with Oliver.

"That horrible Oliver Paisley!" Lori declared. "My sister and I often imagined that he and Henri Rasten were vampires. There's something terribly wicked about them."

"You might not have been too far off the mark with your speculations. I doubt that Oliver and Henri are actually vampires, but several generations of Rastens have been involved with the occult."

"I've heard that Henri Rasten practices black magic. That's one of the reasons that I would never marry him. And his twisted friend,

Oliver Paisley, actually had the nerve to claim that I am emotionally disturbed!"

"Oliver is worried about what you might be telling people. He wants to discredit you by claiming that you are an unstable, troubled young woman. It is a technique that has been used for many centuries. The enemies of some great prophets like John the Baptist have attempted to portray them as emotionally disturbed."

"Fortunately, there are persons like you who can see the truth," Lori said.

"In this case, the truth was quite easy to discern."

"Well, I'm glad that Oliver is gone, and I hope that he doesn't come back. Aside from his visit, it's a very nice morning."

"It certainly is," Mikhail agreed. "Did you have any breakfast yet?"

"Yes. I had some milk and cereal."

"Good. We should go to a more secure location. I had planned to suggest that you spend another night on this sailboat, but since Oliver Paisley is snooping around, it would be better for us to find another place for you to stay. The condominium next door to mine is empty, and I have the key."

"Won't anyone mind if I stay there?"

"No. I'm on good terms with the owner of the real estate agency that manages the condominiums. His name is David Xavier; he's my brother. David is a lawyer. At the moment he's attending a convention in Baltimore, Maryland. He'll be back tomorrow. David and his wife live in one of the condos."

"If you're sure that it will be all right with your brother, I'll be happy to stay there."

"Great. As soon as you're ready, we can be on our way."

A sheepish expression appeared on Lori's face. "I guess that I can leave right now. I'm traveling light these days."

As they walked across the docks, Mikhail noticed that Lori seemed uncomfortable.

"Is everything all right, Lori?"

"Oh, I guess that I'm being silly, but I'm a little embarrassed that I'm wearing the same clothing as yesterday; I wasn't able to iron my clothes, and there are some mud stains as a result of going through the swamp."

"You look so lovely that I hadn't even noticed your clothing."

Lori smiled. "Thank you, Mikhail. Would it be all right if I used some of the money that you loaned me yesterday to buy some new clothing today?"

"Of course. It's your money to do with as you please. However, since you're my guest, let me take you shopping today. In fact, we could go into New Orleans right now and do some shopping and sight-seeing."

"That sounds like fun." Lori's eyes lit up with enthusiasm.

When they went out onto the parking lot, Lori glanced back and saw the sign that read "Xavier Marina and Boat Rentals."

"Do you own this place, Mikhail?"

"Yes. I have two boat rental facilities. At this facility we rent daysailers, catamarans, trimarans, jet skis, kayaks, power cruisers, and cruising sailboats similar to mine. About seven miles from here, I have a lakeside restaurant and rental facility where we have daysailers, canoes, paddleboats, and gondolas."

"You and your brother must be wealthy."

"My family is in good shape financially. We're not as wealthy as Henri Rasten, but unlike the Rastens, our money was earned honestly. In addition to my brother, I have a sister who is a florist and bridal shop owner. My parents are retired and now live in Arizona."

They got into the car and drove toward the city.

"I've only gone into New Orleans three times in my whole life," Lori said. "My parents took us to the Audubon Zoo. My favorite things were the Jaguar Jungle and the Komodo dragon's lair. Lysette and I also really liked the Australian Outback exhibit and the African Savanna."

"I haven't been to the Audubon Zoo for several years," Mikhail said. "Perhaps we can go there together someday."

"Sure."

Mikhail drove Lori to the Garden District where they parked and then traveled around on the St. Charles Streetcar. They went to several shops where Lori was able to purchase new clothing and shoes. She changed into one of her new outfits and carried her old clothes in a shopping bag.

Lori was delighted when Mikhail rented a horse-drawn carriage for the return ride to his car.

"I've always wanted to go on a carriage ride!" she declared happily as the horse clopped along a cobblestone street.

Mikhail next took Lori to the Aquarium of the Americas located in a scenic riverfront park. They looked out at the Mississippi River, then went inside to see the exhibits. Lori and Mikhail especially enjoyed strolling through the sunlit tunnel of the Caribbean Reef exhibit where they were immersed in a world of colorful tropical fish swimming through coral formations. In an Amazon Rainforest display they walked past waterfalls and gazed up at tropical birds. In other galleries Lori was fascinated to see large sea turtles and a rare white alligator.

"I have seen a lot of alligators in the swamp, but this is the first white one that I've ever seen," she said.

When they had completed their aquarium tour, Mikhail and Lori wandered over to Jackson Square and went into the St. Louis Cathedral.

"Pope John Paul II visited this cathedral early in his papacy," Mikhail explained as they looked up at the ceiling paintings depicting scenes from the Bible.

"It's a beautiful church. I like those stained glass windows showing the life of Saint Louis."

Mikhail pointed at the statues on the altar. "Because I'm a sailor, I have always especially liked that Our Lady of the Seas statue."

After leaving the cathedral, they went to a nearby restaurant for an early supper. They sat at an outdoor table and had a meal of onion soup, Cajun crab cakes, and baked potatoes.

Lori looked at Mikhail with admiration, aware that he had made a special effort to treat her to a wonderful day.

CHAPTER 8

▼

Just as Oliver stepped into the study, Henri was hanging up the telephone.

"How is the search going?" Henri asked, shuffling through some papers.

"Not much progress so far." Oliver sat in a chair in front of the desk. "We're still checking the local hotels, but no one has seen her. I went to Xavier's coastal boat rental business, and I'm still puzzled about what happened there."

That statement got Henri's attention. "I've never known you to be puzzled by anything, Oliver."

"Today I am. As you know, one of my special talents is that I can look into a person's soul. I can always tell when someone is lying to me, and I punish lies in proportion to the importance of the matter. However, when I spoke with Mikhail Xavier this morning, I found the shutters closed on the window into his soul. I could sense nothing about the man. He seems to be immune to my powers."

"That is puzzling," Henri agreed. "I didn't think that anyone was beyond your powers. This is something that we'll need to investigate. Finding the girl remains our top priority, though. The

Sheriff tells me that the next time she calls her mother, his phone trace should be able to tell us from where she is calling."

"Good. Then I can go and grab her and bring her back here. I still have my doubts, though, about whether this girl is as important as you believe. You know that the messages of spirit guides can be ambiguous. And Tarot cards are notoriously unreliable."

"I know," Henri said. "Last week I went into the city and spoke to Olympia."

"Bah! That woman only practices white magic. Last year I offered her the opportunity to join our coven, and she refused. Why are you consulting with that outsider?"

"She is the most accurate seer that I know. Olympia was able to confirm the message that I first received in a coven meeting two years ago. After I told her about Lori, she said, 'Unless you become the type of man that this maiden would marry, the spirits shall claim you as one of their own.'"

"That was her prophecy!" Oliver exclaimed. "Could it possibly be any more ambiguous? You could get a clearer prediction from some mambo telling fortunes in the French Quarter."

"Olympia's statement is consistent with what the spirit guides have told me during our coven meetings and with my Tarot cards," Henri said. "It is clear that Lori must agree to marry me. She does not have to like it, but she must make the choice freely, even if that choice is made out of fear of what I will do to her and her family if she defies me."

"If her free choice was not necessary, we could simply forge her signature on the marriage certificate and have it approved by one of the judges on your payroll," Oliver said.

"That would be convenient. However, I plan to have an actual wedding ceremony."

"Are you going to have a priest preside over your wedding in a church?" Oliver asked with a smirk.

"I'm going to have a judge officiate at the wedding here in the mansion."

"I never understood why you went to so much trouble to get Pierre Faire to sign that contract obliging his daughter to marry you. For many weeks you used a combination of spells and drugs to muddle his thinking enough that he signed the papers."

"I worked hard to get that contract signed," Henri said. "Pierre Faire had a strong will. Somehow the man eventually found his way out of the mental fog in which I had enveloped him. I still can't figure out how he did it. Unfortunately for him, as a result of regaining his wits, he planned to renounce the contract. It became necessary for him to have a fatal accident."

"But what was the purpose of the contract?" Oliver asked. "That contract would never be upheld in a real courtroom. Only one of your judges in his kangaroo court would uphold it, and those judges would support you without it anyway."

"The contract was supposed to persuade the girl to consent to the marriage. You can see what a great success that idea was. The girl has a strong will like her father. After we capture her, perhaps we could keep her drugged in order to get through the wedding. I also have a spell that will help keep her subdued."

"First we have to find her," Oliver said.

"Yes, but I doubt that she'll go more than a day or two without calling her mother. And, when she does, we've got her."

Mikhail and Lori each had a bowl of mint ice cream to complete their meal. As Mikhail took his last spoonful, he glanced down the street.

"Oh, oh," he said in a low voice.

"What is it?" Lori became nervous, fearing that he had seen Oliver approaching.

"I'm sorry," Mikhail apologized, realizing what she was thinking. "There is no danger."

"Hello, Mikhail." A tall, striking woman with curly blonde hair and sky blue eyes came up to their table. She carried a couple of shopping bags imprinted with the logos of fashionable clothing stores.

"Michelle!" He stood up and gave her a brief hug. "This is a pleasant surprise."

"I'm certainly surprised to see you in town on such a pleasant afternoon. I thought that you'd be off sailing your boat in search of sunken treasure somewhere."

"Well, I have to come into port from time to time in order to check up on you landlubbers."

"And who is this very young lady with you today?" Michelle studied Lori intently, not missing any detail.

"Michelle, this is Lori Faire," Mikhail introduced them. "Lori, this is Michelle Fournier."

"I'm very pleased to meet you, Michelle," Lori said graciously.

"Hello, Lori. You certainly are an attractive girl. Where did you two meet?"

"Lori visited my seaside marina yesterday," Mikhail said.

"Oh, I suppose that you're a sailor, too, Lori. Perhaps Mikhail will appoint you the first mate on his boat. Personally, I prefer to keep my feet on terra firma."

"It looks like you've been doing a bit of shopping, Michelle," Mikhail said, glancing at the bags.

"Yes. I needed to pick up a few things for the Halloween masquerade this weekend at the Rasten estate. You know all about that masquerade, Mikhail; it's the one that every year you refuse to attend."

"I've never been invited, Michelle."

"Well, I've been invited every year, and you could always have come as my guest. I know that your family and the Rasten family haven't always been on friendly terms, but Henri comes to your restaurant at least once or twice a year, so apparently he doesn't feel hostility toward you."

"I hope that you have a good time at his Halloween party. Who is the fortunate gentleman who will be escorting you to the masquerade?"

"I'm just going with my friend Lily Bannister and her parents, Senator Bannister and his wife. Since you won't accompany me, I guess that I'll just have to be a wallflower."

"We both know that there are many men in your social circle who would love to escort you to any party, Michelle."

"Mikhail, I always seem to be starting an argument with you." She kissed him on the cheek. "And, in spite of my brattiness, you're always so nice to me. I truly believe that you are the finest man in Louisiana."

"Thank you, Michelle. I must be the most fortunate man in Louisiana to be in the company of the two most beautiful women in

Louisiana." When they both gave pleased laughs, Mikhail added, "Link, often asks me about you, Michelle. He'll be glad to hear that I ran into you today."

"How is Link?"

"He got a promotion last month. I transferred Link from my coastal marina to my lakeside place and made him the new manager. Jack Sullivan retired, so I needed someone reliable to take Jack's place. Link has been doing a good job holding down the fort for me there."

"Tell Link 'hello' for me," Michelle said. "Oh, and also tell him that I took up golf. The two of you always seemed to enjoy the game so much that I decided to take a few lessons. Last week I joined Nottingham Hills; it's a delightful new country club that Lily Bannister and her parents also joined. Link can come to the club and play as my guest someday. And, of course, Mikhail, I want you and Lori to come as my guests, too."

"Thanks, Michelle. I'll give Link your message. Believe me, he'll be very happy to play golf with you. I'll let you know when Lori and I can stop by the club."

"Marvelous. It's been wonderful seeing both of you."

Mikhail gave Michelle a kiss on the cheek, and she departed with her shopping bags.

"She seems very nice," Lori said, watching Michelle go down the street. "Have you known her for a long time?"

"I've known her for about ten years since we were both students at Loyola. We've dated off and on during that period. For a while, almost everyone that we knew thought that we would eventually get married, but I don't think that we are destined for each other."

"I see." Lori was relieved and pleased that Mikhail did not have a strong commitment to Michelle Fournier.

Mikhail and Lori returned to his car and drove to the condominium complex that was managed by David Xavier. Each condo was separated from the others by terraces, and each condo had its own patio garden. There was a large area of common land in the back that had an extensive garden.

A three-tiered fountain with dancing waters welcomed them as they arrived at the condominiums.

"I like that fountain!" Lori declared as they got out of the car.

"So do I," Mikhail said. "It looks even nicer after dark when the spotlights are turned on."

He took Lori into the fully-furnished condo in which she would be staying and gave her a tour.

"You can get settled in now and relax for a while. If you'd like, in a couple of hours we could go see my lakeside place."

"That would be lovely, Mikhail. I'll come knock on your door later this evening when I'm ready to go."

Mikhail went to his own condo, leaving his cellular phone with Lori for her to use during her stay.

CHAPTER 9

▼

"The maid said that you wanted to see me immediately," Oliver said, hurrying into the study.

Henri looked at him with a lopsided grin. "I just received a call from the Sheriff. Lori called her mother about an hour ago. She was using a cell phone belonging to Mikhail Xavier!"

Oliver's jaw dropped open. "Damn him! He probably had her hidden on his yacht while I was speaking to him this morning. Yet I could sense no deception in him."

"We don't have time now to worry about his apparent immunity to your powers," Henri said. "We need to get the girl."

"Since she's using a cell phone, we can't be exactly sure where he's keeping her. I believe that the yacht is the most likely place."

"I agree. Let's raid his seaside marina tonight at about midnight."

"All right." Oliver pulled out his own cell phone and called several of his men in order to make arrangements for the raid.

"By departing from our boathouse at eleven o'clock, we should arrive at the Xavier marina near midnight," Oliver said to Henri upon completing his calls.

"At that time our raid should attract little attention. As usual, I trust that you'll handle everything with discretion, Oliver."

"Of course. We'll have the girl in custody soon. Since our conversation yesterday, I've been considering how you can keep control of this girl. As you pointed out, Henri, we place her in a stupor for a while using drugs and your spells. That should keep her pacified for the wedding ceremony. However, since her father eventually overcame your spells and strong drugs, we must assume that Lori might break free also. We can't have her running away every week. A more permanent solution is needed for the long-term."

"What do you suggest?" Henri inquired.

"This afternoon I went to see Azetos Cafard, the voodoo bokor who has come to several of our coven meetings. Ordinary voodoo is too entwined with Christianity, but the dark voodoo of the bokors can be useful."

"I hope that you didn't tell that bokor too much about our situation with Lori," Henri said. "Even though Azetos Cafard has attended some coven meetings, I don't know him well enough to trust him."

"I didn't give him any details, and he knew not to ask for any," Oliver assured Henri. "The bokor gave me some puffer fish toxin that interferes with the chemical messages that control movement and feeling. In mild doses, this puffer poison causes tingling in the lips and lightheadedness. However, in larger doses it can place a person in a zombie-like condition. The zombie leads a sluggish existence as the bokor's obedient servant."

Henri laughed with malicious amusement. "I can always count on your ruthlessness, Oliver. You want to turn Lori into a zombie."

"Not really. We would just give her enough of the puffer fish toxin to keep her under control."

"We'll keep that option available. Until her recent flight from this estate, I had anticipated converting Lori to our beliefs and bringing her into the coven. However, now that she has come under the influence of Mikhail Xavier, it is even more unlikely that she will ever share my beliefs. It might be necessary to use the puffer fish poison to place Lori in a zombie-like state. I will not like it, but I'll do what is needed to save myself."

At eight o'clock that evening Mikhail and Lori arrived at his lakeside business. A wedding reception was being held there, so there was a crowd milling around. Some guests stayed in the cabana-style restaurant with its wicker tables and chairs. Ceiling fans contributed to the tropical atmosphere.

Other guests sat outside at the tables near the lake. Multi-colored lanterns hung in a long line along the white, aluminum roof that protected the outdoor tables from rain and sun.

While Mikhail greeted the bride and groom and their parents, Lori studied on the wall the framed drawings and diagrams of gondolas. Although the text was in Italian, she was able to translate a few words. Lori liked the atmosphere of this place.

Mikhail touched her gently on her shoulder. "Let's take a look outside."

"Okay."

A band was playing softly on the pier, and many couples were dancing.

"Here are the rest of my boats," Mikhail said, waving his arm to include the boats at the docks and the ones out on the lake. "The gondolas and paddleboats are the most popular. Only one canoe is being used at this time, and I don't see anyone sailing. The daysailers and canoes are used more during the daytime."

"With both this place and your seaside marina, you certainly own a lot of boats, Mikhail."

"Yes, just trying to keep my count of boats up-to-date keeps me busy."

"I'd imagine," she said and then added with a shy smile, "Those gondolas look very romantic. Could we go out in one later?"

"Sure."

"Hi, Mikhail." A pleasant-looking man in his thirties approached them.

"Hi, Link. I'd like for you to meet Lori Faire." Mikhail turned toward her. "Lori, this is David Linkletter. Everyone calls him 'Link'."

Lori shook hands with Link. "I like your nickname."

"Thanks. Some years ago I used to play a videogame call 'Legend of Zelda' in which the main character was named 'Link.' I played the game so much that people began to call me 'Link' instead of 'Linkletter'."

"And now you like to play on the golf links," Lori quipped. "This afternoon I heard that you are a golfer."

"Lori and I ran into Michelle Fournier while we were in the Garden District today," Mikhail said. "Michelle said to tell you 'hello', and she wants you to play golf with her someday out at the Nottingham Hills country club. She recently joined that club. Her friend, Lily Bannister, is a member there."

A broad grin appeared on Link's face. "Are you kidding me, Mikhail?"

"No. Michelle really wants you to come to the club as her guest. Lori can testify to my truthfulness."

"That's what Michelle said," Lori giggled.

"That is great!" Link exclaimed, then added as an afterthought, "Michelle was your girlfriend for a long time, Mikhail. Is it all right with you if I go out with her?"

"Yes. It's fine with me, Link. I think that you and Michelle will make a good couple."

"Speaking of couples, I'd better go see if the wedding party needs anything."

"Link, there's one more thing before you go." Mikhail looked around to make sure that no one else was within hearing distance. "Lori is attempting to avoid Henri Rasten. If Oliver Paisley or any of Henri's other goons come around here asking questions, it would be best if you forget that you've seen Lori."

"Lori? Lori who? I've never met any Lori in my entire life."

Mikhail chuckled. "Good man!"

As Link hurried away to attend to the wedding guests, Lori and Mikhail sat down at a lakeside table where a waitress brought them soft drinks.

"That was romantic, Mikhail," Lori said. "You did the work of a matchmaker tonight."

"I was just the messenger boy; however, I think that there is a good chance that the relationship between Michelle and Link will succeed."

"I believe that some romances are destined to occur," Lori said.

"I agree," Mikhail said. "Let's take that gondola ride now." He signaled to the waitress.

Cheryl Kubek, a trim woman in her twenties, returned to their table. "What do you need, Mikhail?"

"Cheryl, you mentioned to me last week that you'd like occasionally to work as a gondolier. How about getting some practice tonight by taking Lori and me out on a gondola?"

"Sure," Cheryl replied with enthusiasm. "I'll be back in a minute."

While Cheryl went to get her gondolier's hat, Lori and Mikhail walked along the dock and got into a gondola on which some wedding guests had recently taken a ride on the lake.

Lori looked out upon the lake waters, which reflected a rainbow of colors from the many hanging lanterns as well as the white moonlight. Upon seeing its reflection, she peered up at the nearly-full moon. Surely romance must be a matter of destiny, Lori thought. If I could choose to be anywhere, I would choose to be on this lake on this night with this man. Surely the hand of Providence has lifted me up and placed me where I am meant to be.

Oliver Paisley and four men took their watercraft ashore a short distance from the Xavier coastal marina. It was just after midnight as the men ran unseen along the deserted beach and up onto the docks. Like rattlesnakes entering a rabbits' den, they moved with silent precision.

First, they struck in the marina office. Tomas Nyssa, the night manager, had been adding up the day's cash receipts when, suddenly, attackers sprang upon him. Although taken by surprise, Tomas gave them a good fight. One assailant lost two teeth; another had his nose broken.

Ultimately, though, Tomas was overcome. A tall and wiry fighter named Jesse managed to knock Tomas to the floor. Jesse kicked Tomas twice in the chest, knocking the breath out of him.

The other attackers grabbed Tomas and tied him to a chair and gagged him. Oliver led the men back out onto the docks. They went onto the sailboat that Oliver thought belonged to Mikhail.

Jesse and another man opened the cabin doors and descended the steps. A quick inspection of the cabin revealed that it was empty.

"There's no one aboard," Jesse said as he came back up the steps.

"I'm not certain that this is Mikhail Xavier's sailboat," Oliver said. "Let's search the other boats with cabins."

For the next fifteen minutes Oliver, Jesse, and the other men carefully searched all of the cruising sailboats and power cruisers large enough to accommodate an overnight passenger. No one was aboard any of these larger boats.

The snakes had come, but the den was empty. Once again their prey had eluded them. Again she was running free.

CHAPTER 10

▼

At about eight o'clock in the morning Mikhail received a phone call from Brendan McKenna, the day manager at the seaside marina. When Brendan had arrived at work, he had been startled to find Tomas Nyssa bound and gagged.

By the time that Brendan came into the marina office, Tomas had managed to free his legs, and he was working intently on loosening the ropes on his upper body.

"What happened?" Brendan asked as he untied Tomas.

"Five guys robbed us. It was a little after midnight. I guess that I should have had the door locked, but we've never had any problems in the past."

Brendan gave him a handkerchief to clean the blood from his nose. "How badly are you injured?"

"Not too bad. I think my nose is broken and maybe a couple of ribs. And I'm going to have to pay my dentist a visit. I lost two or three teeth."

"I'm sorry that this happened to you, Tomas," Brendan said and then called the police and Mikhail. As soon as the police arrived and saw the numerous bruises on Tomas, they summoned an ambulance.

Tomas allowed the paramedics to examine him and to tape his broken ribs, but he refused to go to the hospital.

Mikhail came rushing into the office and was relieved to see that Tomas did not have any life-threatening injuries. Tomas told Mikhail about the overnight raid.

"They got all of yesterday's cash receipts, Mikhail. And they were out on the docks for a while. I could see them going into some of the boats. They probably stole some stuff."

"Probably," Mikhail agreed.

After the police had departed, Mikhail explained to Tomas and Brendan that the intruders had likely been looking for Lori Faire. Mikhail quickly brought the two men up-to-date about Henri Rasten's pursuit of Lori.

While Brendan helped Tomas get safely home, Mikhail immediately headed back to the condominiums. He was anxious to get there to protect Lori.

Henri and his men are apparently aware that she has connected with me, Mikhail realized. *My home address is not a secret; my address is even listed in the telephone directory.*

As he pulled into the condominium parking lot, Mikhail saw his brother, David Xavier, carrying a suitcase across the lot. David resembled his younger brother, except David was heavier and had curlier hair than Mikhail.

"Welcome home, David," Mikhail said as he approached.

"Hi, Mikhail." David set down his suitcase. "I'm glad to be home."

"I want to hear about your trip, but there have been some developments here about which you need to know." Mikhail told David everything that had happened from when he rescued Lori from drowning to the raid on the marina.

The two men knocked on the door of the condo in which Lori was staying, and she let them in. Mikhail introduced Lori to his brother.

"I hope that it is all right with you that I am staying here," Lori said to David.

"Yes, I'm glad to have you here. Mikhail explained the situation to me, and I agree with the decisions that he made. My brother is known for his good judgment."

"And my brother is known for being generous with his compliments," Mikhail said. "Lori, last night some men sneaked onto the docks at my seaside marina and searched the boats. We're assuming, of course, that these were Henri's men." Seeing her worried expression, he quickly added, "If they are searching at the marina, they don't know that you're staying here. However, since they've established a connection between us, we're going to need to keep you concealed until this matter is resolved. We can't go on any more excursions in public for a while."

"I can keep myself amused here, Mikhail," Lori said. "This is a lovely place. Can I continue to go into the garden and park area out back?"

"That should be fine," Mikhail said. "That area is not visible from the street."

"Good."

"We always have an armed, uniformed security guard on duty here at the condominiums, Lori," David said. "I'll advise him to be especially vigilant for any suspicious persons."

"That's good too." Lori's smile returned. "I feel safe here."

"You will be safe," Mikhail promised.

After conversing for a few more minutes, David and Mikhail each went to his own condo. Lori settled herself on the couch and picked up the book that she had been reading before the men arrived.

Having had no breakfast, Mikhail ate an early lunch and read the newspaper. He then went out into the backyard where he was pleased to see some dragonflies and butterflies fluttering around the patio gardens and the lawn.

Mikhail did some warm-up exercises, stretching and then his tae kwon do forms and kicks. To conclude his workout, he went through some tai chi movements and some fencing footwork drills.

Mikhail sat down on a white, wrought-iron bench. While he relaxed there, the sound of children's voices caught his attention. Through a few trees and bushes, he could see several small girls and boys playing with a jump rope. As they jumped, they recited a sing-song chant:

> "*Kingdoms of darkness,*
> *Kingdoms of light.*
> *Guided by angels*
> *Of power and might;*
> *Once in deep Heaven a great war was fought,*
> *And now to the earth, the battle is brought;*
> *On a holy vessel, you must now sail;*
> *For the sake of the Maiden, you must prevail.*"

At first Mikhail did not pay much attention to their chant. Then, when they repeated the verses, he took notice.

That is the oddest rhyme for children to be reciting, he thought. He rose from the bench and moved through the light shrubbery toward the children. They were only out of his sight for a matter of seconds, but when he came around a bush, they were gone.

Where could they be? He walked around another row of bushes; no one was there, though. Hearing the telephone ringing in his condo, he trotted back inside, still puzzling over the mystery of the disappearing children.

Mikhail and Lori had dinner with his brother and sister-in-law in their condo. David's wife, Sandra, was an excellent cook who had once worked at the lakeside restaurant and at a couple of restaurants in New Orleans. She served shrimp remoulade and golden-fried beignets with powered sugar.

"These beignets are delicious," Lori said.

"Sometimes beignets are called Creole doughnuts," Sandra said.

"Beignets are one of Sandra's specialties," David told Lori. "We stopped by the supermarket on our way home this afternoon."

"David and I went into the city in order to visit some of the antique stores and art galleries on Magazine Street," Sandra said and went to get some of their purchases to show their guests.

A short while later the two couples played a game of Trivial Pursuit. Just before ten o'clock Lori and Mikhail said good-night to their hosts. Mikhail escorted Lori through the patio gardens until they reached her patio. They sat down next to each other on a bench and looked up at the stars.

"In his novel, *The Silmarillion*, J.R.R. Tolkien has a legend about Earendil the Mariner who sailed an enchanted ship that could travel the sea of stars. Earendil carried with him a holy jewel called a Silmaril that shone so brightly that it could easily be seen on earth. Those who beheld it in the sky called the Silmaril the 'Star of High Hope'. His wife, Elwing, would watch from a high tower and sometimes use her own mystical powers to join Earendil on his ship as this great captain fought against evil forces." Mikhail pointed up at an especially luminous star. "Look! That could be Earendil's ship!"

Lori laughed and gave him a playful nudge. "That's Regulus, silly. Regulus is the brightest star in the constellation of Leo the Lion. It's 72 light years from earth."

"Maybe, but I still think that might be Earendil," he kidded her.

"You had better hire me as your navigator, Mikhail. You're going to get lost if you try to do celestial navigation."

"Okay. You talked me into it. You certainly know your stars, Lori."

"My family's cottage is so far from the city lights that we get a good view of the night sky. Lysette and I have some binoculars, and we're going to buy a telescope someday. I've read a few astronomy books, but I need to take some college classes in order to learn a lot about astronomy."

"What is that book that you've been so intently reading all day?" Mikhail asked.

"I'm reading one of the books that I borrowed from your bookcase. It's a biography of Saint Joan of Arc that was written by Mark Twain. He considered it to be his best book. I was happy to see that you had this book because I have a special interest in Joan of Arc. Last year I read the autobiography of an ice skater named Tara Lipinski who felt great devotion to Saint Therese of Lisieux 'the

Little Flower'. Tara believed that Saint Therese helped her gain the strength to win an Olympic gold medal. I decided to find my own favorite saint. After I read my book on the lives of the saints, I selected Joan of Arc as my special saint."

"Joan of Arc is one of my favorites, too," Mikhail said. "She was a remarkable young woman. I once saw a good movie about her on television. She was two years younger than you when she led the French army to victory."

"When I was running away through the swamp and didn't know what to do next, I asked Saint Joan to help me and my family." Lori said in a confiding tone.

"Perhaps Joan of Arc was the guide who led you to me," Mikhail said.

"I don't know whether it was my guardian angel or Saint Joan or both of them who brought me to you, Mikhail, but I'll be forever grateful to whoever brought us together."

They spoke for a few more minutes before Mikhail kissed her on the cheek and returned to his own condo.

Meanwhile, David was closely watching a car that had parked on the lane at the front of the condominiums. A man had been sitting in the car for almost an hour.

"Is he still out there?" Sandra asked her husband.

"He's still there." David continued to look through the blinds on the front window. "Call the security guard and have him find out what the guy is doing out there."

While Sandra made the phone call, David went over and opened the front door. He stood in the doorway and stared over at the mysterious car. The driver brazenly stared back, apparently unconcerned that his presence had been noticed.

David stepped outside, but the watcher remained where he was. Just as David had planned, though, the driver was so distracted by David that he did not see the security guard approach the car from the rear.

Jesse Thurman was startled when the guard tapped on the car window. Reluctantly, Jesse rolled down the window.

"What do you want?" Jesse asked sullenly.

"You have been parked on this lane for about an hour," the guard said. "Are you visiting someone in the condominiums?"

"Yeah. I'm waiting for somebody."

"Who?"

"It's none of your business," Jesse said and glared at the guard. He observed that the guard was a large man who wore a holster with a handgun.

"I'm going to have to ask you to move this car."

"This is a public street, and I'm staying here for as long as I want."

"Actually, this is a private lane that is owned by the real estate agency that manages the condominiums." The guard pointed at the nearby street. "That is the public street."

Jesse muttered an obscenity, started the car engine, and drove over to the street where he parked in a spot that gave him a good view of the condominiums.

David went back into his condo and called Mikhail, who had looked out his own window when the guard was speaking to Jesse. Mikhail and David formulated a plan to confuse Henri's spies.

Jesse remained in his parking spot on the street for about a half-hour and then drove away and did not return that night.

CHAPTER 11

▼

By eight o'clock in the morning Jesse's car was back in the same parking spot on the street. Jesse slouched in the driver's seat as he resumed his surveillance. He seemed half-asleep until the front door to Mikhail's condo opened.

Jesse became fully alert as he watched Mikhail and a young woman emerge from the condo. Mikhail carried a suitcase.

Jesse had never seen Lori in person, but he held a photograph of her. He glanced down at the picture, then looked up at the young woman with Mikhail. She was wearing sunglasses and a golf cap. The girl is trying to conceal her identity, Jesse thought; she must be Lori Faire.

After placing the suitcase in the trunk, Mikhail and the young woman got in his car and drove away. Jesse almost immediately followed, keeping a block behind them in an attempt to avoid being spotted.

Mikhail drove into New Orleans and eventually pulled into the parking lot of a hotel in the Garden District. Jesse parked on the street and watched Mikhail and the woman go into the hotel lobby.

As soon as they were in the lobby and out of Jesse's sight, the woman removed the golf cap and sunglasses.

"Thanks, Cheryl," Mikhail said to the waitress who had worked at his lakeside restaurant for five years and was his newest gondolier. Cheryl Kubek was two inches taller and four years older than Lori, but their body build and appearance was close enough to pull off the deception.

"I'm glad to help, Mikhail. I'll see you later," Cheryl said, then walked briskly out the hotel's side door and got into a waiting car.

Link, who was driving the car, had earlier dropped Cheryl off a short distance from Mikhail's condo, and Cheryl had walked across the common ground and entered the condo through the patio door. Link and Cheryl now drove back to the lakeside restaurant.

Mikhail checked into the hotel under the names "Mr. and Mrs. Mikhail Xavier". He paid for a room for the rest of the week. Still carrying the suitcase, he took the elevator up to the seventh floor and went into his room.

Mikhail placed the golf cap and sunglasses on top of the dresser. He set the suitcase on a bed and emptied the contents, which consisted mainly of clothing borrowed from his sister-in-law..

He sat down and watched television for an hour. Then he left the room, made sure that the door was securely locked, and placed a "Do Not Disturb" sign on the hallway doorknob.

Mikhail went down to the lobby and departed from the hotel by the same door that he had entered. He got back in his car and drove away.

Jesse did not bother to follow him. Using his cell phone, he called to give his boss an updated report.

"Mikhail Xavier just left by himself. The girl is probably up in the hotel room. Do you want me to go into the hotel?"

"No," Oliver Paisley said. "Stay where you are for now and keep watching. Mr. Rasten and I are discussing the situation right now. We'll probably make a move this afternoon. I'll let you know."

Later in the afternoon Sheriff Randy Heimos and Deputy Lee Sharpton showed up at the hotel and demanded to be allowed to inspect the seventh-floor room. They claimed to be searching for an emotionally-disturbed runaway girl. Although they were out of their jurisdiction, when they assured the hotel manager that they could get a court order, the manager reluctantly opened the door for them.

"The runaway girl doesn't seem to be here," the manager said after they entered the room.

"No, but her clothing is here," the Sheriff said. "She'll be coming back."

They left the room with the manager, who relocked the door and walked away.

"Let's check the gift shop and coffee shop downstairs in the lobby," the Sheriff said to his deputy. "Jesse Thurman didn't see the girl leave the hotel, but he might have missed her if she went out another door. If we don't find her downstairs, we'll need to keep this room under surveillance until she returns."

They headed toward an elevator.

An hour later the telephone in Mikhail's condo rang.

"Hello?" he answered the phone.

"Mikhail, this is Cheryl. I thought that you'd want to know who is here right now. Henri Rasten just asked me if you would be stopping by and said that he is anxious to speak with you."

"I'll be right there, Cheryl."

Mikhail immediately drove to the lake. As soon as he entered the cabana restaurant, Mikhail scanned the room. He quickly spotted Henri seated at the bar slouching over a drink. Mikhail sat down on the adjacent stool.

"Good day, Henri. It has been a while since I've seen you."

Henri looked over at him. "Hello, Mikhail. I'm glad to see you. Is there anything new in your life?"

"Oh, every week seems to bring new surprises." Mikhail noticed two rough-looking men seated at a table, sipping drinks and surreptitiously watching them. He wondered how many other men Henri had nearby.

"That is true," Henri said. "It has certainly been an eventful week for me. My executive assistant, Oliver Paisley, mentioned to me that he has told you about the young runaway from my estate."

"Yes, Oliver told me. I hope that everything turns out well for the young lady."

"Your concern is touching, Mikhail."

"Well, I try to be a compassionate person, Henri. Sometimes wealthy young men such as ourselves with plenty of spare time and plenty of money can become self-centered egotists. We need to remember that the world doesn't revolve around us. We should do what we can to help others."

"Your attitude is refreshing, Mikhail," Henri said with just a hint of sarcasm. "By the way, are you still dating Michelle Fournier?"

"We haven't dated for a while."

"I thought that you might be dating another girl. Someone told me that he saw you yesterday with a beautiful girl with brown hair. Michelle, as I recall, is quite blonde."

"Some ladies change their hair color periodically. I happened to run into Michelle yesterday in the Garden District."

Henri took another sip of his drink. "I am anxious to find the girl who ran away, Mikhail. Two years ago her now-deceased father signed a legal contract obliging her to marry me when she turned eighteen. However, because the girl is very emotional and becomes upset easily, I decided to wait until she was slightly more mature before marrying her. Now that she is nineteen I feel that it is time to oblige her to honor the contract."

"I'd suggest that you have your lawyer reconsider the legality of that contract, Henri. Forcing someone into an involuntary marriage is almost like slavery."

Henri was taken aback by so direct a reproof.

"Several decades ago, Mikhail, our grandparents negotiated an agreement that we would not interfere with each other's business activities. Your family could do what it wanted in your territory, and we could do what we wanted in ours. It was a good agreement, and it has held for many years. One of the reasons that I stopped by today was to obtain your assurance that you plan to continue to honor the agreement and not interfere with my personal life or business activities."

"I am a peaceful man, Henri, and I try to avoid trouble."

"Good. Then there should be no problems between us."

"I would hope not because I've had enough trouble lately," Mikhail said. "Some thugs invaded my seaside marina last night and beat up the manager. I've discussed the incident with the night manager, and he and I are willing to overlook this attack if there are no future incidents."

"Would you like a drink, Mikhail?" Link asked as he walked behind the bar.

"No thanks, Link," Mikhail said. "Have you happened to see my cell phone today?"

"No, I haven't seen it, Mikhail."

"Well, I don't have it with me. It has been a couple of days since I've used it. Don't worry about it. I'm sure that it's around someplace."

Henri stood up. "I should be leaving now. I need to resume my search for my fiancee."

"Based upon what you have told me, the best thing for everyone would be for you to stop searching for this young woman," Mikhail advised. "Both you and the young woman will be happier if you simply let her go."

"If I could, I would," Henri said. "A good Catholic boy like yourself could never understand my predicament, Mikhail. I must marry this girl soon or I will be destroyed by supernatural forces."

"Henri, I know that several generations of your family have been involved with the occult, but you do not have to continue that involvement. The occult only has as much power over you as you give it. You can always reject it and walk away. You can even become a good Catholic boy yourself."

Henri gave a bitter laugh. "I think not. Power is my birthright, and my power is increasing. I expect your help in returning Lori Faire to my estate. If she is not in my mansion by midnight tonight, there will be dire consequences."

Henri turned and walked out of the restaurant. His two men at a table lingered for several minutes, then departed.

Mikhail, Link, and Cheryl discussed the situation. They decided to post armed guards overnight at both the lakeside business and at the seaside marina.

Mikhail brought home two dinners from the restaurant for himself and Lori. When they had completed their meal, Mikhail got out his chessboard.

Six years ago Lori's father had taught her how to play chess, and she was a good player. Lori fought Mikhail to a draw in both games that they played.

While Mikhail went into his kitchen to get some sodas, Lori examined the wall decorations. She looked at two attractive paintings, then noticed a framed document that appeared quite old. Just as she started to read the document, Mikhail returned with their drinks.

"What is this, Mikhail?" Lori asked.

Mikhail appeared pleased that she was interested in the document. "That is a letter written in 1830 by my great-great-great-grandfather to my great-great-great-grandmother." Mikhail took the framed letter off the wall and placed it next to the chessboard on the table. "My ancestor was a captain in the United States Navy."

Lori read over Mikhail's shoulder while he was reading the letter aloud:

My dearest Rachel,

It has been too many months since I have seen you and our son. During my ship's voyage through the Caribbean, I have gathered numerous unique seashells for Lawrence to add to his collection. For you, my dear wife, I have purchased some religious statues crafted with fine detail and three paintings that capture some of the beauty of this region. You will be able to see the lovely tropical scenery that I am seeing without having to make the arduous voyage!

Two weeks ago our ship met up with a school of dolphins. The playful creatures swam alongside us for many miles before heading east toward deeper ocean. Last week we were fortunate to see a blue whale. The graceful power of this majestic beast reminded us all of the grandeur of God's creation.

Even though there are many wonders in the seas, I would prefer to be at home. The campaign against the pirates is going well. In the last month we have defeated three pirate ships off the east coast of Florida. For some days now we have been in pursuit of a particularly swift pirate vessel. We chased them around the southern tip of Florida and are currently headed north through the Gulf.

These pirates are unaware that they are leading me home to New Orleans! I hope and pray that I will soon see you and our dear son.

Your devoted husband,

William Xavier

CHAPTER 12

▼

Lori gave her full attention to every sentence of the letter. When he had finished reading the letter, Mikhail handed it to Lori so that she could examine it more closely.

"That was William Xavier's last letter to his wife," Mikhail said. "His ship caught the pirate ship near New Orleans, and they fought a tremendous battle."

"Both ships became mired in the mud of the inland waterway through which I escaped on the jet ski," Lori continued the tale. "The two ships destroyed each other by firing their cannons from point-blank range, then the two crews fought with swords and guns in waist-high water. Every man from both crews was killed in the battle."

"I'm pleased that you know so much about the event," Mikhail said.

"My mother told Lysette and me about the battle."

"Several years ago I sailed into the waterway and came close to the spot where the shipwrecks would have been. However, my electronic depth finder indicated that the water was becoming too shallow for me to proceed any further into the waterway. The inlet abruptly changes from being fairly deep to very shallow. The keel on the bottom of my sailboat would have become stuck in the mud. Modern electronics gave me an advantage that Captain William Xavier did not have in 1830. I was able to turn my sailboat around in order to head back toward the Gulf."

"When you were in that waterway, you were probably less than a mile from my family's cottage. I know that area real well. There are all sorts of interesting plants and animals."

"It sounds like a great place to explore. I should have gone ashore and taken a look around."

"Well, you have to be careful. There are some sinkholes. And quicksand. You also have to watch out for the alligators. And there are some snakes."

Mikhail laughed. "On second thought, it's probably just as well that I didn't go ashore."

"A person probably should have a guide if he's not familiar with the swamp. Lysette and I know the area so well that we feel safe wandering around there."

"Perhaps someday you can give me a guided tour."

"That would be a lot of fun," Lori said. "I would very much like to show you around. If that horrible Henri Rasten didn't live so close to the swamp, we could go there and explore."

"The Rasten empire is going to fall someday, and I hope that day comes soon."

"My friend, Joan of Arc, was a great warrior in the battle between good and evil. I'm going to ask her to pray for the defeat of Henri Rasten and Oliver Paisley." She paused and added with a smile. "And for the triumph of Mikhail Xavier!"

Mikhail returned the smile. "Well, I'll certainly be glad to have Joan of Arc fighting on my side."

It was ten o'clock that night when someone knocked on the front door of the Faire's cottage.

"Who would come calling at this time?" Lysette asked, turning off the television as she rose from the sofa.

"Stay there! I'll get it." Jacqueline moved toward the door. She looked through the peephole, but it was too dark outside to identify the visitor. "Who is it?" she asked in a loud voice.

"It's Oliver Paisley, Mrs. Faire. May I come in?"

Her nervousness increased. "It is rather late for us to be receiving visitors, Mr. Paisley. Please come back some other time."

"I fear that my business cannot wait, Mrs. Faire. Please open the door."

"I'll call you on the phone tomorrow morning. Good-night." Jacqueline walked away from the door and turned off a lamp. "It's time for us to go to bed now, Lysette," she said in a voice loud enough for anyone outside to hear.

Then, to her horror, the front door lock clicked, and the door swung open. Oliver pulled the key out of the lock and returned it to his pocket as he stepped into the room.

"How dare you!" Jacqueline exclaimed. "How dare you enter my home without my permission?"

Oliver gave her a patronizing smile. "Actually, Mrs. Faire, this cottage belongs to Henri Rasten. I serve as his representative, and he has authorized me to enter the cottage."

Two other men walked into the cottage and stood behind Oliver. Jacqueline had previously seen the two men on the estate, but she did not know their names.

"What do you want, Mr. Paisley?" she asked, keeping her voice steady.

"Mr. Rasten would like for you and your daughter, Lysette, to stay up at the mansion for a while," he said.

"Why?"

"He thinks that it would be best for the two of you to live there until your other daughter returns. These two gentlemen and I will help you carry your luggage up there."

"We don't want to go to the mansion," she said.

"You have no choice in this matter." His eyes narrowed. "We can do this in a nice and friendly way or we can do this the hard way. That is your choice."

Jacqueline stared at him. She had no doubt that this man and his henchmen would drag her and Lysette away if they refused to go with them.

She turned to her daughter. "Lysette, go pack your suitcase. We'll probably be staying at the mansion for at least a few days."

"Yes, Momma," Lysette said and went back into the bedroom that she shared with Lori.

While the three men waited in the living room, Jacqueline went to help her daughter pack in the bedroom.

As Jacqueline and Lysette were being escorted along the trail that led up to the mansion, a cabin cruiser was pulling out of the Xavier seaside marina. The boat was fully stocked with fishing gear that the two couples aboard planned to use on a three-day trip. No one noticed the speedboat that lurked a half-mile from the marina.

The fishing boat headed southwest into the Gulf of Mexico. Brian Lamb, the 53-year-old businessman who had rented the boat, opened a wine bottle for his wife and their guests. The fish could wait until morning; tonight they planned to celebrate.

When they reached the island that was their destination for the first half of their trip, Brian steered the boat into a cove and dropped anchor. The speedboat had followed them across the Gulf, always keeping at least a mile away from the fishing boat in order to avoid being seen.

Now the speedboat gradually moved closer. It traveled in ever-shrinking circles like a shark feeling out its prey before striking.

Shortly after midnight, Jesse decided that the time was right and told the man at the wheel of the speedboat to head directly toward the fishing boat.

The four occupants of the fishing boat were so preoccupied with their late night party that none of them even noticed the speedboat until it had pulled along the starboard side.

"Ahoy!" Jesse called out, giving a sidelong glance at the two men with him in the speedboat, knowing that they would be amused by his use of the nautical term.

Brian stood up, startled by the arrival of the speedboat. His wife and the other couple stared in surprise at the newcomers.

"What do you want?" Brian asked.

"We want to come aboard."

"Who the hell are you? You shouldn't be sneaking up on people in the middle of the night."

Jesse and one of his men boosted themselves over the starboard railing.

"What are you doing?" Brian demanded. "I didn't give you permission to come aboard my boat!"

"Oh, is this your boat, Captain? We were under the impression that you rented it from Mikhail Xavier's marina."

"How did you know that?"

"We're just real smart," Jesse said and his men snorted with laughter.

"I want you to get off this boat!" Brian took a step forward.

Jesse raised the handgun that he had been concealing at his side. He fired twice, hitting Brian in the chest with the shots. Brian's wife and their guests screamed in horror.

"Shut up!' Jesse ordered.

Brian's lifeless body lay on the deck. Jesse reached down and took Brian's wallet from his pocket. Jesse and the man who had come aboard with him then took all the money and jewelry from the three remaining passengers.

"Now get aboard that rowboat and get out of here!" he gestured toward the dinghy attached to the cabin cruiser.

The three terrified passengers obeyed and were soon floating in the rowboat. They stared up at the men who had pirated their vessel.

"The only reason that I'm leaving the three of you alive is to carry a message back to Mikhail Xavier for me," Jesse said. "Tell Mikhail that a man is dead because Mikhail did not mind his own business. Tell him that more people are going to die if he does not return another man's property."

After delivering his message, Jesse and his comrade turned on the engine of the cabin cruiser and sailed away. They each grabbed a wine bottle and filled the night with raucous laughter as they drank greedily. The man in the speedboat followed them out into the Gulf of Mexico, and soon both boats were out of sight.

CHAPTER 13

▼

Brian's wife and their two guests rowed the dinghy onto the beach of the island. They soon found a local resident, who called the Coast Guard. After the three survivors gave the Coast Guard a description of the attackers and the stolen boat, a patrol boat took the three persons back to the Xavier seaside marina.

Brendan McKenna was the manager on duty at the time and was shocked to hear about the murder of one of their customers. After receiving a call from Brendan, Mikhail went over to David's condo, and the two brothers rushed to the marina.

They consoled the three victims, who then went to a hotel to rest. Mikhail and David had no doubt about who was behind the attack, and they told the Coast Guard officers about their dispute with Henri Rasten and about the threats that Henri had made.

Mikhail had always had good relations with the Coast Guard. The officers promised to investigate and to increase patrols near the marina.

Mikhail and his brother went to David's law office in order to discuss strategy. They had only been in the office for a few minutes when Sheriff Randy Heimos and Deputy Lee Sharpton arrived.

"What can I do for you, Sheriff?" David asked.

The Sheriff placed a photograph of Lori on the desk. "Have you seen this girl?"

"Yes," David said. "Her name is Lori Faire. Henri Rasten is attempting to force her to marry him against her will. She fled from his estate, and Henri Rasten has Oliver Paisley and his other hired thugs out looking for her."

The Sheriff glared at David. "Well, you got the girl's name right, but you have all the other facts mixed up. This girl is an emotionally-disturbed runaway, and Mr. Rasten is trying to help her."

"Henri Rasten and Oliver Paisley are spreading those lies," David said. "I have met Lori Faire; she is an emotionally well-adjusted, highly intelligent young woman."

"Where is she?" the Sheriff demanded.

"She is safely hidden from Henri Rasten."

"This girl is being sought by the police! If you don't tell me where she is, you could be arrested for obstruction of justice!"

David pressed the intercom button on his telephone. "Caroline, could you step in here for a moment?"

She immediately appeared in the doorway. "Yes, Mr. Xavier?"

"I'd like for you to call my attorney. Sheriff Heimos is considering bringing criminal charges against me and my brother. I want my attorney to explain to him what the consequences will be if he does so."

"Now hold on a second!" The Sheriff became rattled. "That won't be necessary," he stammered. "We can work something out."

"Caroline, let's delay that phone call," David said. "However, I'd like for you to have a seat over there and remain as a witness for the rest of the conversation."

Caroline sat in a chair near the door. The Sheriff looked back at her uneasily. He was accustomed to being able to bully people. Now he sat in the office of a man whose family's wealth and power was comparable to that of Henri Rasten.

"Sheriff, you should be aware that a murder occurred last night and that Henri Rasten was responsible for the murder," Mikhail said. He then told the Sheriff and Deputy about the murder of Brian Lamb and the pirating of the cabin cruiser.

"That's all very interesting, but what happens at sea is the concern of the Coast Guard, not mine," the Sheriff said. "I am only concerned with finding Lori Faire."

"Lori Faire is nineteen years old and has a right to go where she pleases," Mikhail declared. "There is no need to search for her. I can assure you that Lori is alive and well and happy."

"Sheriff, my brother and I plan to go to federal authorities," David said. "If you are part of Henri Rasten's crew, now would be a good time to abandon ship. You and your deputy could be granted immunity from prosecution if you testify against Henri Rasten."

"The only criminals in this room are you and your brother!" the Sheriff bellowed. "I am not hiding a runaway teenager!"

"We give sanctuary to those in need," David said. "Sanctuary is an ancient and respected tradition."

"It is not respected by me." The Sheriff and his deputy stood up as they prepared to leave. "I have spoken to Mr. Henri Rasten's lawyer, and his lawyer assures me that Lori Faire can be forced to return to the Rasten estate."

"I am certain that his lawyer can find nuances within the wording of the law that he can twist and distort to his advantage," David said. "The devil speaks with a subtle tongue."

"His lawyer always wins his cases," the Deputy interjected. "The two of you had better watch out."

"His lawyer only cares about winning, not about the truth." David looked up at a portrait hanging on the wall. "I hung that picture of Sir Thomas More on the day that I established my law offices here. He is the paradigm of what a good lawyer should be, and I can look at his portrait to remind myself that the law needs to be based on truth."

"You and your brother will regret hiding that girl!" the Sheriff shouted and stormed out of the office with his equally-enraged deputy.

"Neither the Sheriff nor his deputy would be admirers of Saint Thomas More," Caroline said, still seated in her chair across the room. "If they had lived during that period of history, they would have been supporters of the villainous Henry VIII instead."

"I doubt that either the Sheriff or his deputy will go to the federal authorities," David said.

"Well, you gave them a chance," Caroline said. "Let us hope that, after reflecting on what you told them, at least one of them will change his mind."

Mikhail looked admiringly at Caroline. He had always liked David's secretary: she was a smart, cute woman with a great sense of humor. Mikhail might have asked her out on a date one day if he had not fallen completely in love with Lori Faire.

An hour later, when Mikhail stopped by the condo in which Lori was staying, he found her upset. She had received a call on Mikhail's cellular phone from Oliver Paisley. He had informed Lori that her mother and sister were going to be forced to stay at the Rasten mansion until Lori returned. Oliver had hinted that they would be harmed if Lori did not return soon.

"David is at the FBI offices right now." Mikhail tried to calm her. "We're going to obtain the help of federal authorities in moving against Henri Rasten."

"That might take too long," Lori said.

"We might be able to organize a rescue mission. Tonight, though, I need to go out onto the Gulf with several of my employees to help protect our customers in their boats."

"Be careful, Mikhail." Lori appeared quite worried.

"I will be," he promised. "I've taken steps to increase our safety on tonight's mission."

When Mikhail described what precautions he had taken, Lori relaxed somewhat.

"Henri Rasten and Oliver Paisley don't know that you are staying in this condo, so you should be safe here tonight," Mikhail told Lori. "I would guess that Henri's men are still occasionally checking on that hotel room that I rented. David and Sandra will keep a close watch on this condo tonight. In fact, Sandra is taking a nap right now so that she can remain awake all night. And, as usual, the armed security guard will be on duty outside on the parking lot."

"I'll be fine, just bring yourself safely home." Lori moved forward into Mikhail's arm and pressed her lips against his, kissing him tenderly.

At eight o'clock that evening Mikhail and several of his long-time employees gathered on the parking lot of the seaside marina. Mikhail opened the trunk of his car and pulled open a large box.

"I have a present for each of you." He gave a bulletproof vest to each of the four men. "I purchased these this afternoon, and I want you to wear the vests tonight. The vests are yours to keep."

Link and Brendan McKenna immediately put on their body armor. Tomas Nyssa had some difficulty getting the straps attached properly, but soon had the vest comfortably fitted on his upper body. Even though Tomas had been injured two nights earlier, he had insisted on participating in tonight's operation.

"Thanks for the vest, Mikhail," John Terry said. "During the two years that I was with the New Orleans police, I would always wear my bulletproof vest. It would sometimes get a little warm with it on, but I liked the feeling of safety that it gave me." John was easily the tallest man in the group. He usually worked at the seaside marina; however, he would occasionally substitute for Link as the manager of the lakeside restaurant and boat rental business.

"Are the weapons ready, John?" Mikhail asked.

"Yes. I've loaded them aboard both boats."

"Good work."

The five men walked onto the docks. Mikhail, Link, and John got into a sailboat that was slightly larger than Mikhail's personal sailboat. Brendan and Tomas boarded a powerboat that could achieve fairly high speeds.

A couple with two children had rented a sailboat for an excursion to an island where they planned to do some snorkeling and take some photographs. Tomas and Brendan planned to follow the family's sailboat in order to ensure that these customers had a safe trip.

Link, John, and Mikhail had a different mission.

"I hope that Henri Rasten doesn't send out his men tonight, but if he does, I'd rather that his men attack our boat rather than our customers' boats," Mikhail said. "This high mast will make our sails visible from a long distance, so we might be able to lure the attackers toward us."

"Why aren't we going in your personal sailboat, Mikhail?" Link asked.

"There are three reasons. Some of Henri's men have seen my sailboat, and they might recognize it and realize that we are setting a trap. Secondly, we might have a need for speed tonight, and this boat has a more powerful engine. Thirdly, the hull of this boat is thicker, so bullets are less likely to penetrate into the cabin."

"And, fourthly, Mikhail doesn't want any bullet holes in his personal sailboat," John said jokingly.

Mikhail laughed. "The last time that I checked, I also owned this sailboat. Let's try to keep the bullets out of this boat, too."

The parents and two children departed from the marina on their snorkeling and photography trip. Brendan and Tomas soon followed as the family's protectors. About a minute later Mikhail turned on the sailboat's engines and headed out into the Gulf of Mexico.

When they were about a half-mile from the marina, Mikhail turned off the engine as Link and John hoisted the mainsail and jib.

"Have you called Michelle yet?" Mikhail asked Link.

"Not yet. I'm going to call her next week to accept her invitation to play golf at the Nottingham Hills Country Club. Since Michelle will be going to the Halloween masquerade this weekend, I decided to wait until next week to call her."

At that moment the idea occurred to Mikhail that the Halloween masquerade at Henri Rasten's mansion could serve as the ideal distraction during which a rescue mission could be staged. While over a hundred guests wander around the party that evening, Mikhail and his team could slip into the mansion and rescue Lori's mother and sister. The masquerade would begin in about forty-six hours, so they had sufficient time to formulate a plan.

For now, though, I need to remain focused on tonight's operation, Mikhail reflected. He turned the wheel, steering the boat toward the island where last night's attack had occurred.

Link looked through some binoculars as he scanned the sea for boats. John made some adjustments to the sail trim, then raised a spinnaker sail that featured a bright fleur-de-lis design. The boat's speed increased noticeably with the help of this third, billowing sail.

"I'm going to take us into the cove on the lee side of the island," Mikhail said.

"Do you think that Henri Rasten's men would attack again at this same island this soon?" Link asked.

"Most criminals don't possess much imagination. I wouldn't be surprised if they launched another attack here tonight. In any case, this place is as good as any to set a trap. If nothing happens here, we can try a different spot later tonight."

Their sailboat entered the cove, but they did not drop anchor because they needed to be able to move on a moment's notice.

"I'll take the first watch," Mikhail volunteered as midnight approached.

Neither John nor Link wanted to sleep, though. The three men considered playing cards, but they were too much on edge, so they decided to just sit and talk.

About forty-five minutes after arriving in the cove, they heard the distant hum of a boat's engine. Link raised his binoculars, aiming them in the direction from which the sound was coming.

"There's a motorboat traveling without lights," Link reported. "Only the moonlight enables me to see it."

"These could be Henri's pirates coming to steal this sailboat," John said.

Link and John picked up automatic rifles while Mikhail started his boat's engines. In anticipation of battle, all three men felt a rush of adrenalin.

"The motorboat has changed its course away from us," Link said. "They are apparently trying to avoid being seen."

"Now that's interesting," Mikhail said. "It makes me wonder what they are doing. Let's find out."

Mikhail pushed the engines to full speed as quickly as possible, moving to intercept the motorboat.

"I would bet a thousand dollars that these guys are drug smugglers," John declared as the motorboat adjusted its course again.

When Mikhail continued his pursuit, the three men aboard the motorboat became angry and headed directly toward the sailboat, firing a submachine gun at Mikhail's boat.

When Link, John, and Mikhail returned fire with their own weapons, the motorboat made a sharp turn, increased speed, and went roaring away into the darkness.

"That boat is too fast; we could never catch them," Link said.

"We don't need to catch them," Mikhail said as he went down the steps into the cabin. "I'm going to call the Coast Guard and give them the motorboat's location."

Five minutes later Mikhail came back up onto the deck. "The Coast Guard was alarmed to hear that those men fired on us. They are sending two patrol boats to try to intercept them."

"You have a lot of bullet holes in the hull of this sailboat, Mikhail," John said, looking over the port railing.

"Don't worry about the boat. Just keep yourselves out of the path of the bullets."

They remained in the cove for another half-hour, then sailed away from the island.

"Let's go see how Brendan and Tomas are doing," Mikhail said and headed toward the smaller island where the two men were standing guard over the family who had rented a sailboat from the Xavier marina.

It took Mikhail's boat over two hours to reach the island, and they saw no other boats along the way there. They soon found the couple and their two children, who had anchored the sailboat and were now camping in tents on the beach. On the water a quarter-mile away, Tomas and Brendan served as sentinels keeping a diligent watch from their own boat.

"Things look pretty quiet here," John said.

"That can change in a hurry." Link once again picked up his binoculars to search for any potential threat.

"We might as well circle the island." Mikhail guided the boat on a course that kept them a constant distance from the shore.

They had only traveled about a half-mile when a speedboat came racing toward them. All three men instantly knew what was happening. Mikhail, John, and Link grabbed their rifles.

As Jesse and his two crewmen drew nearer, they were startled by the sight before them. They had expected to find some nearly-helpless victims like the previous night, not three men with armaments equal to their own.

"Surrender and we will not open fire on you!" Mikhail shouted toward the speedboat.

His offer was not accepted. Jesse bellowed threats and obscenities at Mikhail, then began shooting. As the other two men in the speedboat also opened fire, Mikhail and his two friends returned the fire.

A bullet from John's rifle hit Jesse's ear, and a second bullet went through Jesse's forehead. As he died, Jesse toppled backward into one of his crew, knocking the man off-balance.

Seeing their leader fallen, the other man panicked and veered the speedboat away from the sailboat. However, Brendan and Tomas had heard the gunfire. Before the attackers could make their escape back out into the Gulf waters, Tomas and Brendan came charging in, bringing their boat alongside the speedboat, their guns aimed at the two men, who promptly dropped their own guns and surrendered.

Mikhail called the Coast Guard, and in about fifteen minutes, a cutter arrived. Lieutenant Eric Alton and his crew handcuffed and placed the two prisoners aboard the cutter, along with Jesse's body.

"We had our own gun battle less than two hours ago," Lieutenant Alton said. "When one of our patrol boats went to intercept that motorboat that you called to report, they shot at our patrol boat, which returned fire. Just like in this incident, one man was killed and two others were captured. We searched their motorboat and found a large shipment of cocaine and heroin."

"I believe that the three men in the speedboat that we fought here work for Henri Rasten," Mikhail said. "They are likely the same men who killed Brian Lamb last night. I suspect that the drug smugglers whom you captured also work for Henri Rasten."

"We will conduct an investigation to determine if Henri Rasten can be connected to the drug smugglers," Lieutenant Alton said. "His name has been mentioned in past conversations with drug enforcement agents, but the DEA agents have never been able to make a case against him. Perhaps by offering these men that we captured a reduced sentence in exchange for their testimony, the federal prosecutor will be able to indict Henri Rasten."

Mikhail, John, Link, Brendan, and Tomas spoke with Lieutenant Alton and the other Coast Guard officers for a few more minutes, then they returned to the seaside marina.

"Good work tonight, gentlemen," Mikhail congratulated the four men as they walked across the docks. "We helped prevent an illegal drug shipment from getting into the United States, and we successfully defended our customers on their cruise."

CHAPTER 14

▼

Henri Rasten was in a bad mood the next morning. He had received a report about the arrests and deaths on the Gulf of Mexico overnight. More importantly to him, Lori continued to elude his men, who were unable to find where Mikhail Xavier had her hidden. Henri usually enjoyed his annual Halloween masquerade, which was scheduled for tomorrow evening, but this year it was a nuisance.

I will have to waste a lot of time today and tomorrow preparing for that stupid party, Henri thought glumly. Perhaps I'll give Olympia a call; the seer might have some news for me. I asked her to devote special attention to my situation.

Henri went into his office and made the telephone call to Olympia. He was pleased when she answered promptly.

"Have you had any additional insights regarding my future and my relationship with Lori Faire?" Henri asked with some unease. One never knew what a seer was going to say.

"Yes," she replied. "I had a vision last night. I saw you standing on the Gulf Coast beach at dawn, watching the sunrise. Then a huge, winged figure emerged from the horizon and flew across the sky toward you. He was an angel carrying a three-pronged spear. As he flew over the beach, he smote you with the trident, then continued on inland on some other mission. The angel hovered over the waterway and seemed to be waiting for something or someone."

Henri considered Olympia's words. "I believe that I can interpret your vision. One of Lucifer's angels touched me with his trident in order to bestow upon me the powers that I deserve. He was not destroying me; he came to empower me."

"I can tell the difference between an angel from Heaven and a devil from Hell," Olympia said. "We cannot choose to interpret visions to mean whatever is most favorable to us. A vision means what it means."

"Well, what do you think the vision means, seer?" Henri snapped.

"Both the vision and the earlier prophecy are a warning to you. You are being give a chance to reform your life. If you do not repent, you will be destroyed."

"You would be wise not to antagonize me, woman!"

"You can go down to the beach and try to stop the tide from coming in. Order it not to come in. Your odds of stopping the tide are as good as your odds of stopping the fulfillment of prophecy."

"You do the best that you can," Henri said. "I'll give your prophecy all the consideration that it deserves. Let me know when you have something useful to say, Olympia."

Henri hung up the telephone. *Oliver is correct in his assessment of that woman,* Henri thought, still annoyed by her analysis of the vision. *Olympia is worthless.*

Henri went into the dining room, where Oliver was finishing his lunch.

Oliver looked up from his nearly-empty plate. "You look worried, Henri. Losing that cocaine and heroin shipment last night was a severe blow, but we can make up the loss with future shipments. And even though two of our men were killed and the others captured, we can find replacements for them soon enough."

"I don't give a damn about losing the drug shipment or the men," Henri said harshly. "Time is running out. I must marry that girl soon."

"Now that she knows that we have taken her mother and sister into our custody, she will likely surrender to us."

"If we don't have Lori in our possession within three days, I am going to be forced to kill either her mother or her sister. We'll inform Lori of the execution and tell her that the survivor will be killed the next day if Lori does not come back here."

"That strategy could be counter-productive, Henri. We can wait. I feel that our web is starting to close on the girl."

"It is not closing fast enough. Would it be more effective to kill her mother or her sister?"

"If such drastic action proves necessary, I would favor killing the sister and telling her that her mother will be next unless she surrenders herself."

"Yes, I agree," Henri said.

"You realize, of course, that Lori will hate you for the rest of her life if you kill either of them," Oliver pointed out.

"I no longer care how she feels about me. At this point I'm simply trying to avoid being destroyed by the prophecy."

"Nevertheless, it will be unpleasant to live with a wife who despises you."

"I don't intend to do so. We will have Azetos Cafard, our dark voodoo bokor, administer a large dose of the puffer fish toxin to Lori. After she is placed in a zombie-like condition, she won't be able to feel any emotions. She won't bother me at all."

"That plan could succeed." Or it might not, Oliver added silently to himself.

Oliver watched Henri leave the room, pleased that Henri had become so completely committed to the service of Lucifer.

Lori was shocked to hear about the overnight gun battles. One bullet could have ended Mikhail's life and her hopes for their future together.

It was noon as she sat on a couch in Mikhail's condo, conversing with David and Mikhail.

"I am concerned about the safety of my mother and Lysette," Lori told them. "Perhaps we could make a deal with Henri Rasten that, if he allows my mother and sister to return to our family cottage, I will go back to the cottage, too. I'll pretend to be considering his offer of marriage, but I'll tell him that I need a week to reach a decision. Then, when he lets his guard down, my family and I could escape through the swamp." She grinned impishly. "We might even be able to steal three jet skis from his boathouse, but it would be easier if you came to pick us up in your boat."

Mikhail shook his head. "Henri might agree to that deal on the telephone, but once you returned to his estate, you would be his prisoner. He knows how easy it is to slip away into the swamp and then onto the inland waterway. Henri would either force you to stay in his mansion or he would post armed guards near your family's cottage."

"Mikhail is correct," David said. "We can find another way to free your sister and mother. I have been talking to both the FBI and the DEA, and both federal agencies have promised to help. They are both gathering evidence against Henri Rasten. I would expect an indictment within two weeks."

"That won't be soon enough," Lori said anxiously. "I can sense that my mother and sister are in mortal danger."

"I think that Lori is correct," Mikhail said. "I'm glad that the federal government is helping us, but the government does not move swiftly. We need to get her family off that estate as soon as possible. The Halloween masquerade on the Rasten estate tomorrow evening would be our best opportunity to rescue them."

"It might be possible to sneak into the party disguised as guests or as caterers," David said. "The question is how closely will Henri Rasten's staff be checking the identities of persons who come to the masquerade."

"You wouldn't be able to get past his security at the front gate," Lori said. "The only way to get to his mansion would be to take a boat along the inland waterway, walk through the swamp, and then enter from the rear of the estate. There won't be any security guards back there."

"I'm going to take a little drive past the Rasten estate this afternoon in order to get the lay of the land," David said. "Then we can decide how to proceed with the rescue operation."

"Don't take any chances, David," Mikhail advised. "Our family is now at war with Henri Rasten."

"Don't worry," David said. "I am a cautious man."

David Xavier was also a patient man. It was a virtue that had served him well all of his life. For three hours that afternoon he sat in his car patiently watching the front entrance of the Rasten estate.

After finishing his conversation with Lori and Mikhail, David had driven out to the estate. He traveled along the main road and the country lanes that ran near Henri Rasten's property. When David had done as much scouting as he could by car, he drove back to the main road and parked about one hundred yards from the front gates.

A high fence ran along the portion of the estate's boundaries that David was able to survey by car. David had noted the numerous security cameras mounted atop poles just inside the fencing.

From his vantage point, he could see everyone coming and going through the main entrance. Two armed guards stopped and inspected every vehicle entering the estate. A third guard sat next to a telephone in a shack just inside the gates. David speculated about whether the security cameras were monitored in the shack or in a room in the mansion.

Throughout the day several trucks came to deliver supplies for the Halloween masquerade. The guards went into the back of every truck and looked at the contents. The guard in the shack made a phone call every time someone arrived.

David wondered if security was always so tight here or if it had been increased because of Henri's conflict with the Xaviers. Although David would have preferred to have found the estate almost unguarded, he rather liked the idea that Henri Rasten was fearful of their counterstrike.

That counterstrike will not come through the front entrance, David soon decided. We will need to find another way in.

While absorbed in thought about that other way into the estate, he suddenly realized that two guards had walked out onto the roadway and were pointing at his car. David started the engine and drove quickly away, aware that the guards were shouting behind him.

As he headed toward the highway, David continually glanced into his rearview mirror, expecting to see a vehicle in pursuit. However, no pursuer's car appeared, and he breathed a sigh of relief as he merged into the anonymity of the other traffic on the highway.

Later in the evening, David again sat with Mikhail and Lori in Mikhail's condo. David gave them a report about his reconnaissance mission.

"So our best option seems to be to follow Lori's idea about going through the waterway into the swamp and then onto the estate," Mikhail said after David had completed his report. "My team and I will appear to be guests at the masquerade. David, I'll use my cell phone to keep in contact with you in your condo. I'd like for your condo to be our communications center. If necessary, you can contact the federal authorities."

"I'll need to find a costume to wear to the masquerade tomorrow evening," Lori said.

Mikhail was startled. "You're not going!"

"Of course I am," she declared as if there could be no question about her presence on the rescue mission.

"Lori, we need to keep you as far away from the Rasten mansion as possible," Mikhail said. "You can stay here and help David at our communications center."

"Mikhail, I'm sure that you and your team could find your way through the inland waterway successfully," Lori said. "However, after you leave your boat, you'll need to find your way through the swamp. That swamp can be quite confusing if you are not familiar with it. Even with a map and a compass, you could get lost, especially after dark. I probably know that swamp better than anyone in the world; I can be your guide."

"She has a point, Mikhail," David said.

Sensing that she was gaining the upper hand, Lori continued, "And once you reach the mansion, you'll need me to show you around. You have never seen my mother and sister, and I don't have any photographs of them with me. Our family has usually attended the Halloween masquerade, but it is unlikely that Henri Rasten will allow my mother and Lysette to mingle with the guests this year. We'll probably have to search the upstairs rooms, and I know the location of a back stairwell that is seldom used."

Mikhail knew when he had lost an argument. "All right. You can come with us."

"Good." Lori grinned.

After David left in order to make some preparations for the next day's mission, Lori moved closer to Mikhail on the sofa.

"It actually is possible that Henri Rasten will insist that my mother and Lysette attend his party. If he still has the delusion that I am going to marry him, he might consider them to be his future mother-in-law and sister-in-law and want them to attend. The other guests will be his friends and employees; even if my mother and sister explained their predicament to someone, no one from that group would help them."

Mikhail nodded. "Henri has so much control over the local politicians, judges, and police that he might be arrogant enough to allow your mother and sister to attend the party." He then added jokingly, "However, I'm going to assume that they'll be locked away in the bat-filled belfry at the top of a high, dark tower."

Lori laughed. "The mansion has neither bats nor a belfry. You're lucky that I am coming with you."

"The luckiest evening of my life was the evening that I pulled you out of the sea," Mikhail said and kissed her tenderly.

Lori recalled that first evening on Mikhail's sailboat when she had not known much about him. At that time Lori had been concerned that she might have gone from the frying pan into the fire, just like the old saying warned.

Once she had gotten to know Mikhail, her concerns had soon vanished. Now, though, she realized that she had indeed stepped from the frying pan into the fire, and she had freely chosen to take that step. Her passionate love for Mikhail was a fire in which she would joyfully stand for the rest of her life.

CHAPTER 15

▼

The next afternoon, only five hours before they would depart on the rescue mission, Mikhail decided to take Lori on a brief, recreational excursion. Mikhail made the suggestion for the excursion to Lori while they ate an early supper. She eagerly accepted even though he would not reveal their destination.

Mikhail knew that the rescue mission could end disastrously; this might be Lori's only opportunity to participate in this activity that was important to her. First, though, Mikhail went over to David's condo in order to complete preparations for the mission.

"I should go with you tonight," David said. "I need to protect my little brother."

"I need you here, David. This evening, when I'm on the Rasten estate, I'm going to call you from my cell phone and leave the line open all evening. You can record everything that you hear over the phone. If I am captured or killed, you can give the audio recording to the FBI. That should be a sufficient catalyst to get them to raid the Rasten estate. If Lori is captured, you and the federal agents will need to rescue her. The audio recording that you make will ensure that Lori and her family will be free from Henri Rasten regardless of what happens on our rescue mission."

"If your team is detected by Henri's security guards, get out of there immediately, Mikhail," David cautioned. "Then you and I can go together to the federal authorities and present them the audio recording and any other evidence that you gather tonight."

"That sounds like a good plan to me," Mikhail said.

"This condominium will be the scene of two incongruous activities this evening. While I'm in the dining room making a recording of your rescue mission, Sandra will be in the living room giving out candy to the trick-or-treaters. We usually have about thirty kids come by, usually from the other condos and from the houses in the subdivision down the road."

After saying good-bye to David, Mikhail got into his car with Lori.

"We'll be going directly from our recreational excursion to the seaside marina," Mikhail told her. "Do you have your mask and everything that you'll need for the masquerade?"

"Yes, Mikhail, I have everything," Lori said. "Where are we going for our excursion?"

"You'll see."

They drove for about twenty minutes, then arrived at the surprise destination. Lori was delighted to see that Mikhail had taken her to an indoor ice skating rink.

"Oh, Mikhail, thank you!" She gave him a hug.

"You mentioned to me that you enjoyed watching figure skating on television, but that you had never skated on ice. I thought that this would be a good opportunity."

They went inside and rented two pairs of ice skates. It was late afternoon on Halloween, so the rink was not crowded. Lori had previously done some rollerblading with her sister, and she was able to adjust her skating technique to ice sufficiently so that she only fell once. Although Mikhail fell three times, his skating was still better than he expected.

They did a few laps around the rink holding each other upright in the sweetheart skating position. Because they wanted to conserve their energy for the masquerade, they skated for less than an hour. Mikhail and Lori drank sodas at the snack bar, then returned to his car.

They drove to the seaside marina and pulled into the parking lot. Brendan and John had arrived a few minutes earlier and were standing outside of the marina office. Mikhail parked near the building, and he and Lori got out of the car.

"I have one more surprise for you," Mikhail told Lori as he opened the trunk of the car.

"A telescope!" Lori exclaimed upon seeing what was in the trunk. She reached in and lifted up the box. "This is a nice telescope, Mikhail. You're so good to me!"

"Well, I want my navigator to have the equipment that she needs," Mikhail said. "If the sky is clear tomorrow night, we can set it up out on the patio."

Seeing Lori kiss Mikhail, Brendan and John delayed approaching the couple: Brendan began reading the personalized license plates on cars in the lot; John developed a sudden interest in cloud formations.

Lori and Mikhail finished kissing and came forward to greet John and Brendan whose interest in the weather and license plates immediately waned. Mikhail introduced Lori to the two men.

"Here come Link and Tomas." John pointed at a car turning into the lot.

After parking, Tomas and Link walked over to join the group. All the members of the rescue team were now present.

"We went to the bait-and-tackle shop to buy some fishermen's boots and waterproof clothing," Link said. He and Tomas carried large bags filled with their purchases.

"We also bought the two tents that you wanted, Mikhail," Tomas added.

The group engaged in conversation for several minutes and decided to take two boats since they hoped to return with additional passengers.

"I am very grateful that you are coming with us to rescue my mother and sister," Lori told the men. "I know that you are doing so because Mikhail asked you to help."

"We're glad to help, Lori," Link said.

"I've always intended to explore that inland waterway, but I never got around to it," Brendan said. "Tonight will be my opportunity to finally do it."

Everyone gathered clothing, weapons, and gear out of their cars, then walked onto the docks. Each person tugged on waterproof pants and fishermen's boots, reasoning that it would be easier to put the boots on now on the docks rather than in the boats at their destination.

John, Link, Tomas, and Brendan put on their bulletproof vests. Lori was going to wear an evening gown at the masquerade, so she could not wear a vest, and Mikhail found that his tuxedo did not fit over the vest. If the rescue operation went smoothly, there would not be any shooting anyway.

The group was anxious to get underway. At about eight o'clock the two boats departed from the marina and headed along the Gulf coastal waters.

"This motorboat is nice," Lori said. She liked the feel of the cool, moist breeze on her face. "If we weren't on a rescue mission, though, I'd prefer your sailboat. The sails are so attractive when they fill with wind."

This girl is a charmer, John thought admiringly. Link had told John that Mikhail seemed to be enchanted by Lori, and John could now understand Mikhail's fascination.

They soon arrived in the area where Mikhail had first taken Lori aboard his sailboat.

"I wonder whatever happened to my jet ski?" Lori's eyes scanned the beach and shallow water.

"That's a mystery that will likely remain unsolved," Mikhail said.

A minute later their boat reached the confluence of the Gulf of Mexico with the inland waterway. John steered the motor cruiser into the waterway, the powerboat following close behind them.

All was quiet as they traveled along the waterway and past the boathouse from which Lori had taken the jet ski.

Eventually, they reached the point where the waterway merged into the swamp, and they could travel no further by boat. Brendan, Link, Mikhail, and Lori carefully lowered themselves into the waist-high water. They unloaded the waterproof bags containing their gear, clothing, and weapons.

John would remain on board the motor cruiser, while Tomas would stay in the powerboat.

"All right, gentlemen, you have a cell phone," Mikhail said. "When we reach dry land, Link will call you and keep the line open until we return to these boats. I'll use my own cell phone to establish a similar communication link with my brother."

"Our link with be with Link," John declared, causing Link and the others to chuckle at his pun.

"We should be back in less than two hours," Mikhail said.

After Tomas and John wished them good luck, the group moved away from the boat. Lori was familiar with the swamp, so she went to the front into the point position.

"This is the shortest route to dry land," she explained as they waded past some trees into shallower water that was only knee-deep.

From somewhere up ahead, from the woods toward which they were headed, some creature howled.

"I assume that there aren't any werewolves around here," Brendan said, half-jokingly.

"I've never seen one," Lori said.

"You'll notice that she didn't deny that there could be werewolves here," Link said.

"You should worry more about them than about werewolves." Lori pointed at what had appeared to be a log.

"An alligator!" Link exclaimed. "Are there any other dangers here for which we should watch out?"

"Did I mention that this swamp was haunted?" Mikhail asked dryly.

"Perfect," Link groaned.

"Actually a haunted, alligator-infested swamp is almost the perfect place to spend Halloween," Brendan said.

"I'll prefer Halloween when we arrive at the masquerade in the elegant mansion," Link said.

"Yet great evil lurks in that mansion, not in this swamp or woodland." Mikhail stepped out of ankle-deep water onto solid ground.

When everyone was on dry ground, they set down their waterproof bags and took off their fishermen's boots. The men assembled two tents, and Lori went into one of the tents in order to change into clothing appropriate for the masquerade.

Brendan, Link, and Mikhail put on shoulder holsters holding guns, which they concealed beneath their jackets. They stored their boots and waterproof gear in the second tent.

When Lori emerged from her tent, all three men were impressed by her beauty as she stood in a flowing evening gown in the moonlight. Seeing their reaction, Lori was amused and pleased.

"This must be a magical woodland, and you must be the princess who rules here," Mikhail said.

"I am," Lori responded playfully. "Come, my prince, and we shall remove the usurper who challenges my rule."

"I follow, my lady, but first I must speak with my sibling." Mikhail picked up his cell phone and called his brother.

"Hello?" David answered on the first ring.

"Hi, David. We're at our first checkpoint."

"That's great, Mikhail. How is everything going?"

"Fine, so far. We took the boats through the waterway without any problems. Then Lori did a skillful job of guiding us through the swamp. Without her, we would probably be hopelessly lost or flailing around in some quicksand. There seems to be a lot of quicksand around here."

"Don't get caught in any of that stuff," David cautioned.

"We won't. We're safely on dry land now, and we're about to approach the Rasten estate. In fact, we might be on Henri's property right now; I'm not sure where the boundary line to his property begins."

"Well, I've started recording, and I'll continue to do so until you're safely back onto the Gulf waters," David said, "Remember, Mikhail, if you have difficulty finding Lori's mother and sister or if there's too much security at the mansion, you can just regard tonight's mission as a reconnaissance mission. Just return to the boats, and then we can use the information that you gathered to devise a new rescue mission."

"All right, David," Mikhail said. "I'm going to put this phone in my jacket pocket now. I'll keep you informed about our progress."

"Okay. Bye, Mikhail."

Link then called the boats in order to inform Tomas and John that the rescue team was about to approach the mansion. Upon completing his call, he placed the cellular phone into his own coat pocket. Everyone straightened their clothing and put on their masks. They walked forward through the woods toward the dangers that awaited them.

CHAPTER 16

▼

Lori, Mikhail, Link, and Brendan emerged from the trees and quickly walked across the open land toward the glittering lights of the mansion.

Mikhail hoped that no one would spot them until they got closer to the house. Four guests wandering around such an isolated part of the estate would be a strange sight that could raise questions and draw the attention of dangerous men.

Fortunately, the attention of everyone seemed to be directed inward toward the lavishly-decorated mansion and its illuminated veranda. Several limousines were dropping off guests at the front entrance.

The four uninvited guests advanced across the lawn shrouded in darkness. As they approached the rear of the mansion, they could hear music drifting through the open veranda doors and onto the large porch where numerous persons were gathered.

Because several guests had already wandered into the garden area just off the veranda, the foursome were able to merge in with the other guests inconspicuously.

"Well, everything seems to be going according to plan so far," Mikhail observed.

"Remember Murphy's Law," Lori said.

"Oh, Mr. Murphy and I are old friends. I'd be pleased if he decides to visit our host tonight."

Lori chuckled. "It's about time for things to go seriously wrong for Henri Rasten."

Brendan spoke in a low voice to Mikhail. "What should we do now?" he asked excitedly, tapping his heel out of nervousness.

"Let's all stay out here for a while," Mikhail said. "With some luck, Lori's mother and sister could come strolling onto this veranda, and we can simply spirit them away into the swamp. We might never need to go inside."

"Mikhail, you should be elected the president of the Young Optimists' Club," Link said.

"Perhaps." Mikhail smiled and adjusted his mask. "Why don't we get some punch and sit down for a few minutes?"

"Good idea," Lori said.

The three men and Lori went over to the punch bowl on a table in the center of the veranda. They filled their glasses, then sat down in chairs that lined the porch's perimeter.

"This is a good place to discreetly watch the crowd," Lori commented, taking a sip of punch.

There were about thirty persons out on the veranda. They wore a great variety of costumes: Cleopatra danced with Marc Anthony; Shakespeare conversed with Abraham Lincoln; witches, goblins, and ghouls gathered near a buffet table.

Like Mikhail, Lori, and their companions, many guests were dressed in formal evening wear and wore a mask. Most of the masks were made of either velvet or leather; black was the most popular color, especially for the men. Red masks ran a close second for the women, who usually matched the color of their masks to their gowns.

Lori observed one woman whose pink silk masks flourished an elaborate display of peacock feather. "Some of these masks must cost more than their gowns."

"I don't doubt it," Mikhail replied. "I have a great Zorro costume at home, but we need to be as inconspicuous as possible tonight."

Because it was a comfortable temperature outside, the glass patio doors leading into the ballroom were kept open. Mikhail, Lori, Brendan, and Link could clearly see many of the guests inside.

"I'd estimate that there are about seventy persons in the ballroom," Lori said. "At least a few more will be arriving stylishly late."

"Henri Rasten is moving toward the front door again," Mikhail said. "Another important guest must have just arrived."

"I still don't see my mother or sister." Lori peered intently through the veranda doors.

"While Henri is distracted by his new guests, this might be a good opportunity for us to saunter on inside." Mikhail stood up and the others followed his lead. "It looks like we're not going to be able to do this the easy way."

"What do you want us to do?" Link asked Mikhail.

"You and Brendan remain out here. Lori's mother and sister will probably stay together if they are attending this party. If you see two ladies who match their descriptions, approach them casually and introduce yourselves. Then, in return, they'll undoubtedly tell you their names. If they are Jacqueline and Lysette, explain to them what is going on. Link, you can take them down to the trees while Brendan comes inside to get Lori and me."

"You can count on us," Link assured him.

"Good luck, Mikhail," Brendan said.

"Thank you, gentlemen. We'll see you in a little while."

Mikhail offered his right arm to Lori, who wrapped her elbow through it as they strolled off the veranda and through the doors leading into the mansion.

They walked past the jazz band that was entertaining the guests. After getting some hor d'oeuvres and two more glasses of punch, they moved toward a far corner from which they could observe the gathering.

"In spite of their costumes, I can recognize several local politicians and television personalities," Mikhail said in a low voice. "Some of these people are on Henri's payroll and some of them are not."

"Henri must be having this party catered," Lori said. "I don't recognize any of the men or women serving food and drinks."

"If you don't spot your mother and sister in the next couple of minutes, we'll move to the other side of the ballroom."

"I can see most of the persons over there, Mikhail. I don't think that they're attending this party."

"Then let's take that back stairway upstairs. They're probably locked in a room up there, unless he allowed them to return to your home."

"I doubt that he would allow them to leave here. My mother and Lysette are somewhere in this mansion."

"We need to leave the ballroom quickly," Mikhail abruptly declared.

Lori was startled. "What's wrong?"

"Do you see that blonde woman in the pink gown and mask? That's Michelle Fournier. She might recognize me. We'd better head for that stairway immediately."

Lori glanced across the room. "Yes, I think that you're right. Her hairdo is rather distinctive."

While she spoke with Oliver Paisley, Michelle's eyes were scanning the crowd of guests. Since she had arrived at the masquerade, one man after another had been attempting to win her favor. Oliver was her current admirer; she had met him once previously, and he was handsome enough and generous with his compliments, but there was something that she did not like about the man.

Suddenly she spotted a man whom she would recognize even when he was wearing a mask.

"Now that's a surprise!" she exclaimed, interrupting Oliver's recitation of her merits.

"What?" Oliver turned to follow her gaze.

"That man over there is Mikhail Xavier," Michelle said. "I would never have expected to see him at one of Henri's parties. I thought that they disliked each other. And Mikhail seldom goes to any parties even those given by persons whom he likes." Her eyes focused on Lori. "That must be his new, little girlfriend. I suppose that she made him come this evening."

Oliver stared in astonishment at the couple. "I do believe that you are correct, Michelle: that is Mikhail Xavier! And he seems to be escorting Miss Lori Faire this evening!"

"Which of them was invited? I wouldn't think that Henri knows that girl, but I doubt that he would invite Mikhail."

"Oh, Henri has known Lori Faire and her family for many years. They have a standing invitation to all his parties." He started to walk away. "If you would excuse me, I should inform Henri that Lori and Mikhail have arrived."

"Yes, of course," she said, watching him hurry across the ballroom.

When she glanced back, Mikhail and Lori were walking through the swinging door leading into the kitchen.

"Why on earth are they going back there?" she said to herself. "What is going on here?"

Not knowing that they had been spotted by Oliver Paisley, Mikhail and Lori entered the kitchen. The employees of the catering firm ignored them. Lori recognize the mansion's regular cook, but the woman was so busy that she did not notice them.

Lori and Mikhail walked up the back stairwell. Mikhail pulled the cellular phone out of the inner pocket of jacket.

"Hello, David?"

"Yes, Mikhail?"

"I just wanted to do a quick check. Are you able to hear everything that is being said?"

"Yes, the sound is very clear. I could even tell you what the band was playing down in the ballroom."

"Good. We've reached the second floor, so I have to go." After saying good-bye to David, Mikhail returned the phone to his jacket pocket.

Lori and Mikhail exited the stairwell on the second floor. They moved cautiously down the hallway.

Lori knocked on each door and called out softly, "Lysette? Mama?"

Both Mikhail and Lori jumped when, on the third attempt, a door swung open and Lysette stood there gaping at her sister.

"Lori!"

"Lysette!"

As they embraced, Jacqueline Faire appeared in the doorway.

"Lori!"

"Mama!"

"What are you doing here?" Jacqueline asked, hugging her daughter.

"We sneaked into the masquerade party," Lori explained. "Mama and Lysette, this is Mikhail Xavier. He rescued me when I ran away and has been protecting ever since that time."

"Thank you so much for helping my daughter, sir."

"It's wonderful to meet both of you." Mikhail bowed his head politely. "Now allow me to escort you three ladies out of here."

As they started to walk back toward the stairwell in order to return to the kitchen, two large men emerged from the stairwell.

"Run the other way!" Lori shouted to Lysette and Jacqueline. "Go down the grand staircase!"

Mikhail pulled his gun from his shoulder holster. He kept himself protectively between Henri's men and the three women who reached the staircase.

Henri's men advanced menacingly with their own guns drawn. The women descended the staircase, Mikhail lagging behind as a human shield.

By unspoken agreement, Henri's men and Mikhail concealed their guns when they neared the bottom of the staircase. They were within view of dozens of party guests. Mikhail hoped that the old rule about there being safety in numbers would help them this evening.

"Mikhail!" Lori called back to him. "Look!"

He glanced down to the first floor where he saw Henri Rasten and Oliver Paisley waiting near the front door. A large man stood behind them, further blocking that escape route.

CHAPTER 17

▼

With no where else to go, the three women and Mikhail stepped off the stairway into the front hallway. Mikhail looked across the ballroom; he could barely see the open patio doors which led out onto the veranda. He wondered whether Link and Brendan could have seen them coming down the grand staircase. Mikhail doubted it.

He stood directly in front of Henri.

"Well, hello," Mikhail said. "We were looking for the cloakroom, but we seem to have made a wrong turn."

"Good evening, Mikhail," Henri said. "Lori, you look beautiful this evening."

"So much for our clever disguises," Mikhail said, removing his mask.

Lori followed his example; the mask reduced her peripheral vision, and she wanted to be able to see any possible escape route for them.

"You're always ready to make your little joke, Mikhail," Henri said. "Regardless of the circumstances, I'm glad that you brought Lori to me tonight."

"We've had a pleasant evening," Mikhail said. "Your Halloween masquerade certainly deserves its impressive reputation. We have to be running along now, though; we promised to visit another party this evening."

"We are going to need to detain you for a bit, Mikhail. Lori, would you bring your mother and sister with you? We all need to have a private chat in my study."

Mikhail felt a gun equipped with a silencer jammed into his back by one of the men that had come down the staircase. Even if he had been wearing his bulletproof vest, he doubted that the vest would be able to stop a bullet from this point-blank range.

Oliver held Lysette's arm firmly. Mikhail could see the knife that Oliver pressed against her back.

Henri saw where Mikhail was looking. "Lori is the only person in your group who is completely safe. I am fond of sweet, little Lysette and her dear mother, but I will hurt them if you do not cooperate. Carefully pass your gun back to one of the men behind you."

"We are within full view of many of your guests," Mikhail pointed out.

"My guests will simply be told that we were evicting some drunken party crashers. As we toss you out the front door, they won't realize that you have been shot and Lysette stabbed."

Mikhail considered the situation, then handed his gun back to the man with the silenced gun. He would not risk the lives of these women.

As the captors and their captives walked down the hallway toward the study, Michelle watched with trepidation. *That man is holding a gun on Mikhail! What is happening?* With a sinking feeling, she realized that she was responsible for the situation. Why did I tell Oliver Paisley that Mikhail was at the party? Why did Oliver have to be talking to me at the moment I spotted Mikhail? As soon as I told Oliver, he went to Henri Rasten, and then they summoned some henchmen.

Her thoughts continued to race as she strove to avoid panic. Who was the woman and the teenage girl with Mikhail and Lori? They seemed to be prisoners also. Michelle's eyes scanned the ballroom as she sought potential allies. I must undo my mistake, she realized. I must help Mikhail and Lori.

Meanwhile, Lori, Lysette, Mikhail, and Jacqueline stood in front of Henri's desk in his study. Henri was seated, while Oliver and the three armed guards stood at different points in the room.

The cellular phone was still in the pocket of Mikhail's jacket; Henri and his men had assumed correctly that Mikhail had only carried the gun that they had taken away from him, so they had not bothered to search him. Mikhail knew that his brother was hearing and recording this entire conversation. Poor David must be terribly worried, Mikhail realized.

"We could negotiate a new version of the old contract that existed between our families," Mikhail suggested. "If you allow Lori and her mother and sister to leave with me, we won't file any criminal charges against you. And, in future months and years, if you leave us alone and leave my family's businesses alone, we won't cause you any trouble."

Henri grinned sardonically. "That would be quite a good contract for you, Mikhail. I seem to be holding all of the cards. Even if you were to offer me a million dollars for Lori, I would not allow you to leave the estate with her."

"Henri, you can't seem to understand that Lori is a person, not property. She does not belong to you, nor does she belong to me." Mikhail was attempting to stall for time; eventually, Brendan and Link would become worried and enter the mansion.

"I don't intend to debate this matter with you," Henri said sharply. "Jacqueline and Lysette will be returned to their rooms upstairs. Lori will be escorted to her own room upstairs. You will be escorted off this estate by my men."

"You're planning to kill him!" Lori blurted out. "You won't let him leave because you know that he'll never stop trying to get me out of here!"

Henri looked at her sternly. "Calm down, Lori. You're better off with me than with Mikhail. Someday you'll understand that is true."

"I'll hate you forever if you kill Mikhail!" she shouted.

"Keep your voice down." Henri was concerned that she had been heard in the ballroom.

"Henri, I should tell you that we have informed federal agents about our rescue operation tonight," Mikhail said. "Your local gang of crooked cops won't be able to save you."

Mikhail looked toward the high, stained-glass window behind Henri's desk: he thought that he saw someone moving in the dark outside. Were his men about to come bursting through with guns blazing?

"My lawyer can handle your federal friends," Henri said. "And you make a mistake in assuming that I don't have a federal agent on my payroll."

Mikhail pulled the cell phone from the inner pocket of his jacket and held it forward for all to see. "I'm certain that the federal agents listening to this conversation would like to hear the name of the agent that is on your payroll. Speak up, Henri. They're waiting."

Henri was momentarily taken off guard by Mikhail's flourishing of the phone and his revelation that the conversation had been recorded. One of the guards grabbed the phone out of Mikhail's hand and turned off the phone.

"That was a bold maneuver, Mikhail, but it won't do you any good," Henri said. "I can arrange for recordings to disappear from an evidence storage room." Henri motioned to Oliver. "Take two guards with you and get rid of him."

Mikhail again glanced toward the window. If Link and Brendan were out there, they needed to make their move now.

Help came from a different direction. Without a knock, the door to the study swung open and Michelle sauntered in as though it were the most natural thing in the world for her to do so. A young woman and a man followed her into the room.

Hastily, the guards concealed their guns. Michelle completely ignored the guards anyway.

"Henri, what are you and Mikhail scheming about in here?" she insisted to know in a pleasant way. "Everyone at the party is dying with curiosity to know what is going on in here?"

Henri tried to contain his anger. "Michelle, we are having a private meeting. Would you and your friends please excuse us for now?"

"No. Have your meeting tomorrow. Tonight is supposed to be a party. By the way, my two friends here are Lily Bannister, Senator Bannister's daughter. This is her boyfriend, Terry Slayton. I've been telling Senator Bannister what an interesting person Mikhail is, and the Senator wants to meet him."

"My father is waiting for you in the ballroom, Mikhail," Lily said, sounding as if she were reciting a line in a play. Mikhail suspected that Michelle had told Lily exactly what to say.

Michelle wrapped her arm through the crook in Mikhail's elbow. Lily and her boyfriend moved in close to Lori, Lysette, and Jacqueline and escorted them toward the door.

Henri and Oliver stood gaping at what was happening. One of the guards moved to block the doorway, but Henri waved his hand, indicating to the guard that he should stand aside and allow them to pass.

Keeping together in a tight group, they moved through the hallway toward the ballroom.

"Michelle, do you know what is going on here?" Mikhail asked her.

"I only know that I am pulling you out of a hole that I accidentally pushed you into," Michelle replied. "I'm certain that you'll have a wonderful story to tell me once we are safely away from here."

As soon as they entered the ballroom, Mikhail spotted Brendan and Link standing inside the patio doors. He realized that they could not have been the forms that he had seen moving outside of the study's window.

Oliver, Henri, and several of his men followed them into the ballroom, shadowing them as they walked toward the veranda. Henri exchanged a few words with Sheriff Randy Heimos, who then moved toward the patio doors in order to intercept Mikhail, Lori, and their group before they got outside.

"Mr. Rasten tells me that you've been causing trouble here tonight, Mr. Xavier," the Sheriff said. "I might need to arrest you for trespassing. We had best go back to his office and discuss this situation."

Mikhail was about to make a sarcastic response to the Sheriff, then he reconsidered and said instead, "Sheriff, you are a fortunate man: I am going to give you one last chance at redemption. Henri Rasten intends to kill me and keep those women as prisoners against their will. I want to file charges against Henri and Oliver. I can provide you with more than enough evidence to convict them of many crimes."

"The only charges are going to be against you, boy."

"I have already spoken with the FBI. They're going to close in on you this week. If you help me tonight, I'll ask them to go easy on you. I've seen your deputy here this evening, and I have some men of my own here. We could combine forces and arrest these criminals."

The Sheriff paused and seemed to be trying to decide what to do. Mikhail was impressed by how a man's ultimate destiny could rest upon a single decision for good or evil.

The Sheriff glared at him. "I'm telling you for the last time to get back in that office. You are the one under arrest."

Mikhail sighed. "Wrong decision, Sheriff." The threat of imminent action by the FBI had frightened the Sheriff, but not enough to get him to turn against his longtime mentor. "Sheriff Heimos, one of my men is standing behind you," Mikhail added. "He has a gun at your back."

Keeping the gun in the pocket of his jacket, Brendan pressed the barrel against the Sheriff's back. The Sheriff's eyes widened.

They forced the Sheriff to go out onto the veranda. After taking the Sheriff's gun, Mikhail placed it in his own shoulder holster, replacing the gun that had been taken by Henri's men.

"You're in a heap of trouble over this, boy," Sheriff Heimos told him.

"I think not," Mikhail said. "One way or another, your job as Sheriff ends tonight. Thanks for the gun."

Mikhail did not hear the Sheriff's angry response as Mikhail led his group through the guests on the veranda and then off the veranda and through the bushes on the far side.

Lily and her boyfriend remained on the veranda. They later returned to the ballroom where proximity to her father, Senator Bannister, would ensure their safety.

Although Michelle could have remained within the protective aura of the Senator's company, she decided to stay with Mikhail's group. Any jealousy that she had felt about his relationship with Lori was completely forgotten; even though he was no longer her boyfriend, he would always be her dear friend whom she would forever love and respect. Michelle also saw that Link was with Mikhail's group, and Link's presence reinforced her decision to go with them.

CHAPTER 18

▼

The Sheriff, his deputy, Henri, Oliver, and several of their men continued to follow Mikhail's group. However, in order not to alarm the guests on the veranda, Henri's men split up and moved slowly.

Mikhail, Lori, and their group ran across the lawn and into the woods. About fifty yards separated them from their pursuers.

Fortunately, everyone in Mikhail's group was able to run at a good pace. Jacqueline was only in her mid-forties and was in good enough shape to keep up with her daughters, Michelle, and the men.

"I just spoke on my phone to John and Tomas," Brendan told Mikhail. "They're going to start up the boats' engines and take up firing positions in case we have to shoot our way out of here."

"We will," Mikhail assured him.

As they moved deeper into the woods, a mist enveloped them. Mikhail was running next to Lori. He glanced over at Lysette and noted how closely the two sisters resembled each other. Slim and delicate, Lysette seemed to glide through the mist like a fairy.

The ground started to descend gradually, and the mist thickened into a fog. They were getting closer to the swamp.

Perhaps seeing that their prey might actually elude them, the pursuers opened fire. Henri's men had silencers on their guns; however, any sounds bounced off the water vapor, causing the ominous hiss of each shot to be clearly audible to everyone.

The Sheriff had not had time to get a replacement gun for the one that Mikhail had taken from him. Deputy Lee Sharpton, though, fired several shots from his unsilenced revolver, the sound of the explosions seeming to echo for miles through the fog.

"If any of you hit Lori, I'll personally cut your head off and add it to my collection!" Henri shouted at his men.

Knowing that he was not bluffing, all gunfire immediately ceased. Lori was in the midst of Mikhail's group, making it impossible to shoot at any of them without endangering Lori.

All of Henri's men had seen his prized collection of shrunken heads, which Henri had purchased from every continent except Antarctica. Some of the shrunken head were hundreds of years old. None of Henri's men wanted to increase the size of the collection by defying his orders.

Mikhail's group slowed down as they entered into knee-high swamp water. Michelle tripped on a submerged branch and almost fell, but Link caught her arm and steadied her. Knowing that this was her first time in the swamp, Link had been staying close to Michelle in order to protect her and help her.

"Thank you, kind sir," Michelle said, slightly breathlessly. "You are helping my guardian angel do his work tonight, Link. When they were shooting at us a couple of minutes ago, I noticed that you kept yourself between me and the gunmen."

"A gentlemen should do no less for a lady," Link replied with a smile as they splashed their way forward through the water.

Link was surprised that Michelle realized that he had been shielding her. This woman definitely keeps a cool head and her wits about her, he thought admiringly.

Henri and his men remained about fifty yards from Mikhail's group. The Sheriff, being somewhat less physically fit, struggled to keep pace with the rest of Henri's group.

"Are you going to make it?" Oliver asked the Sheriff as the puffing man caught up with them.

"Yes," he replied, trying to catch his breath. "And I'm going to kill Mikhail Xavier when we catch them."

"I'm reserving that pleasure for myself unless Henri decides that he wants it," Oliver said. "We'll allow you to kill one of Mikhail's men, Sheriff. That should satisfy you."

The Sheriff remembered that he would need a gun in order to kill anyone. "Lee, give me your revolver. After we start killing these boys, you can take one of their guns."

Somewhat reluctantly, Deputy Sharpton gave his revolver to the Sheriff, who then placed it in his own holster. The group continued to slog southward through the swamp. Sheriff Heimos soon was lagging about twenty yards behind his deputy. Because he disliked being in the knee-high water, Sheriff Heimos moved up onto a section of higher ground.

He ran for about forty yards before noticing that the ground was not consistently solid. The Sheriff stumbled as he feet became mired. He looked down and was shocked to see that he was trapped in quicksand.

"Help me!" Sheriff Heimos called as he began to sink.

Oliver, Henri, and their men paused, turned around, and saw the Sheriff's predicament. Henri was annoyed by the delay.

"They're going to get away if we don't keep moving!" Henri shouted and then called back to the Deputy, "Sharpton, go pull your boss out of the quicksand and then rejoin us up ahead." With those words, Henri and the rest of his group resumed their pursuit, leaving Sheriff Heimos and Deputy Sharpton behind.

Lee Sharpton picked up a long tree branch and ran back to the Sheriff, who was steadily descending into the quicksand. The entire lower half of his body was no longer visible.

"Grab onto this, Sheriff!" Deputy Sharpton held out the branch.

The Sheriff managed to grab hold of it, but by now the quicksand was up to his shoulders. Because the Sheriff had descended so far, the Deputy could not get much leverage. With a final cry, Sheriff Randy Heimos completely disappeared into the quicksand.

The Deputy stared in shock at the spot where the Sheriff had died. After about ten seconds, he cast aside the branch that he had been holding. Deputy Sharpton looked around and realized that no one else was within sight. He did not like being alone in the swamp at night, and he ran as fast as he could in order to catch up with Henri's group.

While he ran, he kept a close eye on the terrain, not wanting to suffer the Sheriff's fate by stepping into quicksand. He continued to hurry as he went into the swamp water. Deputy Sharpton saw a floating log blocking his path and reached forward to push it aside.

A fraction of a second too late he knew that he had made a mistake, but he could not retract his hand in time.

He hit the side of the large alligator, which reacted with deadly speed. The alligator whipped itself around, its jaws snapping shut on Deputy Sharpton's thigh. The Deputy reached for his revolver, then as his hand touched the empty holster, he recalled with a sinking feeling that he had loaned his gun to the Sheriff.

About seventy yards ahead Oliver and Henri heard someone screaming, but they did not want to take the time to go back to investigate.

"We're getting close to the inland waterway," Henri said to four of his men. "Go to our boathouse and get the jets skis and a speedboat. They must be heading toward some boats that they have hidden nearby. We need to cut them off before they get out onto the Gulf waters."

The four men changed direction, now running east toward the boathouse. Henri occasionally received drug shipments and other contraband at a secret dock near the boathouse; however, because this dock was so close to his estate, he did not risk using it too often to receive these illegal shipments.

While these men went to get the watercraft, Henri, Oliver, and a man carrying a semi-automatic rifle continued the pursuit southward.

Further ahead Mikhail, Lori, Jacqueline, Lysette, Michelle, Brendan, and Link moved into waist-deep water. Everyone in their group was startled as a black, three-foot-long water moccasin wove its way through their midst. The water moccasin brushed against Brendan, but did not strike. As a child, Brendan had nearly died from a rattlesnake bite. Mikhail knew about Brendan's fear of snakes and admired Brendan for volunteering to come on this mission in spite of that fear.

Because of the pursuit, they had not had time to recover the fishermen's boots and waterproof gear that they had hidden in tents in the woods. Even if they had been able to grab the bundles of gear, they could not have paused long enough to put on the waterproof clothing. They were all soaked as they finally arrived at the inland waterway.

CHAPTER 19

▼

To their delight and relief, they heard the sound of boat engines. Seconds later the powerboat and the motor cruiser emerged from the fog. Tomas and John brought their craft to a stop and helped their passengers get aboard.

Mikhail, Lori, and Brendan got into the motor cruiser with John at the helm. Jacqueline, Lysette, Michelle, and Link climbed into the powerboat that Tomas was steering.

The boats turned around in order to move through the waterway and out into the Gulf of Mexico. Everyone took cover when the man with the semi-automatic rifle began firing. He shot at Tomas' boat because he had seen Lori get aboard John's boat.

Several bullets hit the hull of Tomas' boat. Mikhail, Link, and Brendan returned the fire. One of Link's shots grazed the rifleman's ear.

Before the boats had gone even fifty yards, the roar of engines seemed to come from every direction. Three riders on jet skis came charging at the boats, while a speedboat picked up Henri, Oliver, and their rifleman.

A wild and deadly water ballet ensued as Lori, Mikhail, and their companions attempted to break through the web that was closing around them. Visibility was poor in the fog and darkness. One gunman on a jet ski was traveling at high speed and failed to see the low-hanging branch that fractured his skull. He fell into the water and never surfaced.

Another jet ski rider raced ahead of Mikhail's two boats, looking backwards and firing as he passed. Then the gunman's jet ski crashed into a submerged tree root sending the jet ski and its rider hurtling in different directions.

John and Tomas immediately steered their boats away from this obstacle. Henri and his men had temporarily been distracted by the two crashes, but they now resumed their attack.

Their speedboat cut in front of Mikhail's boat, maneuvering to block any escape out of the narrow passage. Henri's rifleman fired at John, and the bullet hit his shoulder. John lost his grip on the wheel, causing the motor cruiser to veer wildly toward the shore. Brendan grabbed the wheel and regained control of the boat.

"I'm all right," John assured them. "The bullet passed straight through my shoulder."

Lori and Mikhail helped lower him to the deck.

"Rest here on the floor, John," Lori said, applying pressure to the wound.

"Something strange is going on here!" Link shouted from the other boat. "I fired six shots at that man!" He pointed at Oliver, who stood unharmed next to Henri, the rifleman, and the other gunman who was steering the speedboat that blocked their passage through the waterway.

"Apparently you missed your target," Tomas said.

"I'm not a good shot, but I'm not that bad," Link said.

"Then he must be wearing a bulletproof vest," Tomas said.

"But he still should have reacted to bullets hitting the vest," Link objected.

"Look!" Mikhail exclaimed, pointing at a spectral light moving amongst the trees. A luminous form came near, almost close enough to distinguish his facial features.

In future weeks and months, there would be much debate about what happened that Halloween night. Was there actual supernatural intervention or had their imaginations run wild, stimulated by local folklore, a full moon, and an ever-shifting fog?

The fog had steadily become thicker, making it difficult for everyone to see what was happening. Lori, Lysette, and Mikhail saw his wings unfold and a three-pronged spear appear in his hand. However, the fog obscured him from the others in their group.

"What's happening?" Lysette cried out.

"What sort of trickery is this, Mikhail?" Henri shouted. "I believe not in your phantasms!"

With a physical prowess that surprised everyone, Henri jumped from the speedboat onto Mikhail's boat. Lori was only inches from the two men, so neither man wanted to risk firing his gun in close combat. They threw rapid combinations of punches and kicks at each other; both Mikhail and Henri had studied martial arts, and both men were proficient.

Meanwhile, Oliver's attention was focused completely on the winged, luminous figure who now stood on the near shore.

"We have been lured into an ambush," the rifleman in the speedboat said to his boss. "They are using special lighting to create illusions." The rifleman did not believe in the supernatural.

Oliver, though, knew exactly what was happening: he could sense the power resonance all around them.

"Pull closer to the shore," Oliver ordered the gunman who was steering the speedboat.

Confident in his power, Oliver decided to challenge this new enemy. He raised his hands and fire sprang forth. Whether this was true mystical power or a trick produced by a magician's illusion, no one watching could ever say with certainty.

However, everyone could see that Oliver's attack failed. When Oliver hurled his fire at the luminous figure, the fire dissipated, falling apart like a loosely-packed snowball thrown into the wind.

The fog became so dense that it obscured the view of Oliver's speedboat.

"This cannot be!" Oliver exclaimed.

Something hit the waterway with great impact, causing a wave that lurched the boats and splashed water over everyone. There was the sound of bodies falling into the water.

When the fog lessened somewhat, everyone could see that the speedboat was empty, its hull wrecked by a gaping hole in its deck. The speedboat looked as though it had been impaled by a giant spear.

Three whirlpools had formed in the water; the fractured speedboat was quickly pulled into the center whirlpool directly beneath it.

Meanwhile, Mikhail and Henri neared the completion of their intense fight. Henri had aggressively thrown many punches and kicks at Mikhail's head, but Mikhail was a more skillful martial artist, and he was able to block and evade most of Henri's attacks, then counter with lightning-fast combinations of roundhouse kicks, side kicks, crescent kicks, hook kicks, and various hand techniques such as the backfist strike.

Henri faked a punch to the head, then caught Mikhail off-guard with a front kick into Mikhail's chest, knocking some breath out of Mikhail. Seeing his momentary advantage, Henri snarled and charged forward.

Until that point in the fight, neither man had used any spinning kicks because the deck was slippery and there was little space to maneuver. When Henri charged toward him, though, Mikhail decided to risk trying a spinning stiff-legged kick.

Mikhail's strategy was successful as Henri was caught by surprise, and it was Henri who slipped on the wet deck as he unsuccessfully tried to evade Mikhail's powerful kick. Mikhail's kick hit Henri's chest with great force, sending Henri reeling into the water.

Near where Oliver had disappeared in the water, the three whirlpools continued to swirl. Now Henri was caught in the spiraling flow of a vortex and dragged beneath the water's surface.

Thinking that some of Henri's gunmen still survived, Mikhail spun around ready to resume the battle. There was no one remaining to fight, though. The battle was over.

CHAPTER 20

▼

For several seconds everyone in the two boats remained silent as they contemplated what had just occurred. They rode the motor cruiser and the powerboat through the waterway and out onto the Gulf of Mexico Link had called the Coast Guard so that a patrol boat would come to meet them.

Mikhail's cell phone was back in Henri's office at the Rasten mansion, so Mikhail picked up one of the cell phones that his men had been using. He dialed his brother's number.

"Hello?" David answered almost immediately.

"Hi, David."

"Mikhail! Thank God! I was afraid that you were dead!"

"I'm fine. In fact, we're all fine, except John was wounded by a bullet that passed through his shoulder. John will be all right, though."

"Where are you?" David asked.

"We're out on the Gulf, close to the inland waterway. Lori's mother and sister are here in the boats with us, and everyone is safe now. Henri Rasten and Oliver Paisley are both dead, and the thugs working for them are dead, too."

David was amazed. "What happened?"

"All Hallows' Eve was an especially holy evening for us this year."

"Thou speakest in riddles, my brother," David said.

"All shall soon be made clear," Mikhail said. "It's a long story, David; I'll tell you everything when I see you."

"I'm going over to the seaside marina now," David said. "I'll meet you there."

As they said good-bye, the Coast Guard patrol boat came alongside the motor cruiser. John was transferred to the Coast Guard vessel and taken to the nearest medical facility. His shoulder wound was sterilized and bandaged. In the morning, he was able to go home.

Early in the afternoon of that next day, due to the shooting and the audio recordings that David had made, the FBI and DEA raided the Rasten estate. Mikhail, David, and Link accompanied the federal agents as they searched through the mansion gathering information about Henri's criminal network.

At about six o'clock that evening Mikhail returned to his lakeside cabana restaurant. The multi-colored lanterns had just been illuminated, and the band was setting up for their performance.

Mikhail stopped at the bar to get a Pepsi before weaving his way through the customers at the outdoor tables until he reached the table where Lori was finishing her supper.

"Hi." He kissed her on the cheek. "Where are your mother and Lysette?"

"They went to buy some clothes. It was sweet of you to give them so much money, Mikhail."

"I was glad to have the opportunity to help," Mikhail said, sitting down across from her. "During the raid on the Rasten estate today, we recovered your mother's and sister's property from the mansion. Then Link, David, and I went down to your house and picked up some clothing, jewelry, photo albums, and some other things. If you want, we can go back tomorrow to get the rest of your stuff."

"That will be fine, Mikhail. Did the federal agents arrest anyone at the estate?"

He shook his head. "The housekeeper and the cook were the only two persons there when we arrived. However, the FBI and DEA agents hit gold during the raid. Henri Rasten's computer files contained detailed records about numerous drug transactions and other criminal operations. The files give the names, addresses, and phone numbers of dozens of Henri's criminal associates throughout Louisiana and the entire country. The federal agents said that they'll be able to capture a lot of criminals as a result of the information that they gained today."

"Great," Lori said.

"An FBI agent named Sanders called me a few minutes ago. He said just received the preliminary coroner's report. They recovered the bodies of Henri Rasten and most of his men. Most of them died from drowning. One of the men had a fractured skull as a result of colliding with a tree branch; the coroner is not yet certain whether he died from the head injury or from drowning."

"What about Oliver Paisley?" Lori asked

"Oliver's body has not been found. There is also a mystery about what happened to Sheriff Randy Heimos and Deputy Lee Sharpton. Apparently, the Sheriff and the Deputy were among the group chasing us through the woods and the swamp, but they are missing and no one knows what happened to them."

"Their evil group is completely destroyed," Lori said. "Now no one will bother us." She placed her hand on Mikhail's. "It was a mysterious and wondrous night."

"I'm sure that we will be reflecting upon the events of last night for the rest of our lives," Mikhail said. "I have had enough excitement for a while, though. I'm hoping that tonight will be much less eventful."

"Let's hope so," Lori said with a laugh. "It's a beautiful, clear evening. Look at all those stars! I can imagine Earendil the Mariner and his wife, Elwing, sailing amongst the stars in their enchanted ship in that J.R.R. Tolkien novel."

"I wish that I could take you sailing in the stars, too."

"You are a true romantic, Mikhail Xavier."

"You inspire romantic thoughts, my dear." He leaned across the table to kiss Lori, who leaned forward to meet him halfway.

At another outdoor table fifty feet away, Michelle and Link were having dinner together.

"When Mikhail, David, and I were on the Rasten estate today, it occurred to me how pointless all of Henri Rasten's criminal activities were; one day he is a wealthy, powerful man, and the next day he is dead," Link said.

Michelle nodded. "Henri worked for years to build up his evil empire, and in an instant, it all falls apart. Most of Henri's money will probably go to the families of persons victimized by his criminal organization. Lori might end up being richer than Mikhail."

Link laughed heartily. "I doubt that will happen. Mikhail is pretty rich."

"Any man with friends like you is rich." Michelle's eyes shone with admiration as she looked at Link. "You risked your life to help him and Lori just because he asked for your help. And, as we ran through the swamp, you shielded me from the gunfire. I always considered you to be an interesting man, and my opinion of you continues to go up."

Link was pleasantly surprised when Michelle kissed him.

"In the last few weeks, I played three of those computer games that you recommended to me," Michelle said. "They were great fun. It was like being transported to another world."

"I'm glad that you took my recommendations," Link said. "A couple of days ago Mikhail mentioned that you have also started playing golf. If your invitation to play with you at the Nottingham Hills course is still open. I'd like to accept."

"Marvelous!" Michelle said with great enthusiasm. "Let's play tomorrow afternoon."

"It's a date." Link returned her smile.

When the band started playing, Mikhail and Lori went out onto the dance floor. They conversed during a slow dance.

"If we eventually decide to get married, I want you to choose me for your husband because I am the sort of man that you want to marry, not because I helped you and your family," Mikhail said. "You should enroll at Loyola University next semester. While you advance your education, we can continue to build our relationship."

"What a dear, sweet man you are!" Lori declared. "Henri Rasten wanted to possess me as his property, but you just want to send me to college!" Lori pulled him closer as they continued to dance. "You're not going to get off the hook that easily, Mikhail Xavier: I'll go to Loyola University next semester, but I plan to marry you someday. Sometime this winter or spring, I'll be expecting you to surprise me with a marriage proposal."

Mikhail laughed as he spun her across the dance floor. He looked out onto the water that sparkled with color from light reflected from the lanterns. A gondola propelled by Cheryl Kubek moved smoothly away from the dock.

I still am amazed by how well everything turned out, Mikhail thought. All my actions were freely chosen by me, and all worked to complete the weavings of patterns too complex for us to understand during our mortal lives.

I once read that music can form a bridge between earth and Heaven, Mikhail recalled as he listened to the band. Tonight, at this moment, I stand upon that bridge.

CHAPTER 21

▼

Seven years later Mikhail placed a letter on the pillow next to his wife in their hotel room in France. The letter read:

My dearest Lori,

I have occasionally added brief notes to the Valentines, birthday cards, anniversary cards, and Christmas cards that I have given to you, but I feel that I owe you a real letter.

I am glad that we brought our daughter with us on this journey through Ireland and France. While we were walking with Lauren along the cliffs and rolling hillsides of County Kerry, I perceived the magic that seems to be infused into the Emerald Isle. I hope that Ireland can provide fuel for Lauren's imagination just as that marvelous, mystical Bayou swamp and woodland stimulated your imagination and that of your sister.

Three days ago, as we sat in our hotel room in the city of Cork, on that rainy evening, I read Lauren some tales from her storybook. Even though the weather kept us inside the hotel almost the entire day, I believe that this was my favorite day of the trip so far. In Lauren's eyes, I could see the leprechauns, pixies, and gnomes engaged in their high-spirited mischief.

Two days ago, while you were in the gift shop purchasing souvenirs for your mother and Lysette, our tour guide told Lauren and me the legend of St. Brigid's Plain. When Brigid asked the King of Leinster for land on which to build a monastery, he said that she could only have as much land as her cloak would cover. Brigid spread her cloak on the ground, and it continued to grow until it covered twelve square miles. Because of his promise, the King had to give her that land for the monastery.

Lori, since the day that we met, my love for you has grown like Brigid's cloak. I frequently thank the angels and saints who served as God's agents in bringing us together. Since arriving in France, Saint Joan of Arc has often been in my thoughts. I truly believe that she helped us after you asked for her intercession.

Tomorrow we shall visit the birthplace of that wonderful girl, and I am anxiously looking forward to seeing her village Domremy.

Next week Link and Michelle will celebrate their five-year anniversary. While we are in Domremy, we should buy a souvenir for little Mikhail. I still have not gotten over my surprise that they named their son after me.

Traveling through life's journey with you is a joy for me.

Your devoted husband,

Mikhail Xavier

The next day Lori arose a few minutes before Mikhail and placed her own letter on the pillow next to him. This letter read:

My dearest Mikhail,

Like you, I am thrilled to be in Domremy, France. Saint Joan of Arc graced the world for an all-too-brief nineteen years, but now she is our friend forever.

As I reflect upon the events of seven years ago, it is startling to realize that our darling Lauren would not exist today if not for the series of events set in motion by Henri Rasten. So much good came about as a result of his wicked schemes!

Of all the kind and noble things that you did during that eventful week, one of the most touching was taking me ice skating before we went on the rescue mission. Because I was so excited to be ice skating for the first time, it did not occur to me until a later date why you had selected such an unusual time for our recreational excursion: you were concerned that, if you were killed and I was captured, I might never again have the opportunity to go skating. You knew that this was something to which I had been looking forward, so you made certain that it would happen, regardless of what happened on the rescue mission.

In a way, it was an act of defiance against the forces that threatened my freedom. Then you gave me my first telescope!

Since, in a few months, I'll receive my Master of Science degree in astronomy, buying that telescope was a good investment. At last I'm fully qualified to do celestial navigation on our sailboat! Even though, as a result of my studies at the university, I have access to much more powerful telescopes, the telescope that you gave me will always be my favorite.

I'm pleased that Lysette will receive her Bachelor of Arts degree in art history on the same day that I receive my Master's degree. When we return from our trip, Lysette wants to paint our family portrait.

Now, Mikhail, let us take Lauren into the town of Domremy. Like me, Joan grew up in a small, simple house, and her family was poor, but not needy.

Although my dear father, Pierre Faire, departed from this world four years before the birth of his granddaughter, I know with certainty that my Poppa watches her and us from Heaven. Every day I recall happy memories from the years when I lived in that cottage in which my spiritual foundation was established.

My family provided me with the paradigm of how to love. Their love for me opened my heart and prepared me to meet you, Mikhail. You are my first love, my true love, my only love, and I am,

Your devoted wife,

Lori Xavier

978-0-595-36291-2
0-595-36291-5

Printed in the United States
52498LVS00006BA/61-90

9 780595 362912